Praise for Bestselling Author Diane Capri

"Full of thrills and tension, but smart and human, too. Kim Otto is a great, great character. I love her."

Lee Child,
#1 New York Times Bestselling Author of Jack Reacher Thrillers

"[A] welcome surprise....[W]orks from the first page to 'The End'."

Larry King

"Swift pacing and ongoing suspense are always present...[L]ikable protagonist who uses her political connections for a good cause...Readers should eagerly anticipate the next [book]."

Top Pick, Romantic Times

"...offers tense legal drama with courtroom overtones, twisty plot, and loads of Florida atmosphere. Recommended."

Library Journal

"[A] fast-paced legal thriller...energetic prose...an appealing heroine...clever and capable supporting cast...[that will] keep readers waiting for the next [book]."

Publishers Weekly

"Expertise shines on every page."
Margaret Maron, Edgar, Antho
Award Winr.

D1059805

JACK
AND JOE

by *DIANE CAPRI*

Published by: AugustBooks
http://www.AugustBooks.com

ISBN-13: 978-1-940768-59-5

Original cover design by Cory Clubb
Interior layout by Author E.M.S.

Published in the United States of America.

Visit the author's website:
http://www.DianeCapri.com

ALSO BY DIANE CAPRI

The Hunt for Jack Reacher Series:
Don't Know Jack
Jack in a Box (*novella*)
Jack and Kill (*novella*)
Get Back Jack
Jack in the Green (*novella*)
Jack and Joe
Deep Cover Jack
Jack the Reaper
Black Jack (*coming soon*)

The Jess Kimball Thrillers Series
Fatal Enemy (*novella*)
Fatal Distraction
Fatal Demand
Fatal Error
Fatal Fall
Fatal Edge
Fatal Game
Fatal Bond (*coming soon*)
Fatal Past (*coming soon*)
Fatal Dawn (*coming soon*)

The Hunt for Justice Series
Due Justice
Twisted Justice
Secret Justice
Wasted Justice
Raw Justice
Mistaken Justice (*novella*)
Cold Justice (*novella*)
False Justice (*novella*)
Fair Justice (*novella*)
True Justice (*novella*)

CAST OF PRIMARY CHARACTERS

Kim L. Otto
Carlos M. Gaspar

Charles Cooper
Lamont Finlay

Eunice Summer
Madeline Jones
Alvin Barry
Jeffrey Mayne
Anthony Clifton
Randy Taylor
Matthew Clifton
Lesley Browning O'Connor
Thomas O'Connor

and
Jack Reacher
Joe Reacher

Thank you to some of the best readers in the world:
James Artem, Sebastian Rochester, Declan Maunder,
Betty Farish Johnston, Lynne Graham, and Delphina Osgood
for participating in our character naming giveaways which make
this book a bit more personal and fun for all of us.

Perpetually, for Lee Child, with unrelenting gratitude.

JACK

AND JOE

THE ENEMY

by Lee Child

1990

Joe and I had started out together, but he had seen the future first, and it had aged him, and worn him down.

I never went back to Fort Bird. Never saw that Sergeant again, the one with the baby son. I thought of her sometimes, when force reduction began to bite. I never saw Summer again either…. Our paths never crossed again.

CHAPTER ONE

Friday, November 19
6:43 AM
Charlotte, North Carolina

THE AIRBUS PILOT ANNOUNCED preparation for landing at
Charlotte Douglas International Airport. I closed my eyes and
gripped the armrests and tensed every muscle in my body, as
usual. I thought about the US Airways Airbus A320 ditched by
Chesley Sullenberger in the Hudson River on January 15, 2009.
The Carolinas Aviation Museum at the Charlotte airport holds an
unparalleled technological lead over other commercial aviation
museums because it exhibits that plane. I hoped our pilot was as
skilled as Sullenberger during our descent through the heavy
black clouds.

The Airbus's wings rocked and we hit the ground with a
hard thud and a couple of bounces, but we made it and I believed
the danger had passed. But you never see the disaster that gets
you.

I gathered my bag, yanked its telescoping handle up and

settled my laptop case atop it, and deplaned through the jetway. I'd taken only a few dozen steps of the long trek to the car rental when the aroma of freshly brewed coffee pulled me to the end of a twelve-deep queue of java hounds.

Travelers hustled past in the usual airport chaos while the coffee line inched ahead. I glanced at my Seiko. Only seven-fifteen.

Just as the customer holding up the line finally moved aside with his triple-shot soy caramel macchiato, the Boss's secure cell phone vibrated in my pocket. His timing was perfect. Which meant he was monitoring my every move, as always. He delivered a new phone at the beginning of every assignment to which only he had access. This one had not rung before, but it was the same phone as all the others, so I knew what it was when I felt it jiggling inside my pocket.

"Otto," I said into it from habit, distracted by the strength of caffeine addiction and my growing proximity to the heavenly brew's source. As if anyone else might answer his phone. Or that he didn't already know my name.

"FBI Special Agent Kim Otto, right?" A woman's voice glazed by the hint of a Southern accent she might have acquired in childhood.

I blinked. How did she know this particular phone was in my pocket? Maybe she was calling at the Boss's request, although he'd never allowed anyone else to call one of these secure phones before.

I pulled the phone down and looked at the display. I was good with numbers and the call was from one I didn't recognize, but that didn't mean anything. Randomizing source call numbers was a snap for the FBI. Which meant it was probably simple for the military, too.

I pressed the phone back to my ear. "Yes." Wary. The phone was as secure as possible, but nothing was one hundred percent secure, especially inside an airport.

"This is Colonel Eunice Summer." She was talking into a speaker. Background noises were present but muffled. "I understand you're conducting a background check for the SPTF."

I blinked again. My cover story was the Special Personnel Task Force background check on Jack Reacher. Colonel Summer was my subject. Her job provided access to high-level classified intel and I was scheduled to interview her today at Fort Bird, North Carolina.

"Yes." I was standing in the middle of an airport terminal surrounded by strangers and subject to data collection by amateurs as well as multiple agencies, foreign and domestic. The very air was literally aware of every transmitted word. The less said, the better.

Summer spoke as if she were aware of the risks but unconcerned. "I've confirmed your assignment with the Chief of Staff. He's ordered me to meet with you and answer all of your questions."

I felt like I'd landed on a different planet. Never during my assignment to build the Reacher file had an interview subject contacted me in advance. Usually, they had to be coerced into speaking to me at all.

"I'm sorry," she said, sounding as if she meant it.

Here it comes, I thought. The excuses. The delays. The refusals. No friend of Jack Reacher's had been willing to tell me anything about him. Some of them wouldn't have answered even one of my questions if their hair were in flames and I was standing two feet away with a fire hose. Why should Summer be different?

"I promised to meet you at ten-thirty in my office in Rock Creek. I've had a change of plans. Hang on."

I heard dead air.

What was she talking about? I looked at my Seiko. It was seven twenty-five already. I couldn't possibly drive to Rock Creek, Virginia, by ten-thirty this morning.

The Boss knew everything. Why had he sent me to Fort Bird if my subject was located four hundred miles north of here?

She came back on the line. "Sorry. Had to pass a slow-moving RV. Honestly, vehicles should stay in the right lane where they belong if they can't keep up on these mountain roads."

"No problem." I frowned and shuffled ahead a few steps in the java line and waited for the coffee and for her to come to the point.

"Something came up. On a corruption case I've been working for a while. I'm driving to Fort Bird, North Carolina. I should arrive in the XO's office about ten o'clock and I'll be there the rest of the day." She paused as if something had caught her attention again. "I don't know where you're located, but if you can come to Fort Bird instead of Rock Creek, we can do your interview there. It shouldn't take long to tell you everything I know and it's all old news, anyway. I haven't seen Reacher in twenty years. Would that work for you?"

"Uh, yeah. I can make that happen. Hang on a minute." I was now at the front of the line and a long queue had formed behind me.

The barista smiled at me and asked for my order. She seemed a little disappointed when I said, "Black coffee, please. The biggest size you've got."

I reached into my pocket for a five-dollar bill just as a hyperactive ten-year-old plowed right into me and knocked me back against my bag.

The bag fell.

I fell on top of the bag.

The kid fell on top of me.

The Boss's cell phone went flying out of my hand.

The kid's twin brother came running to a halt inches away from our pile.

He kicked the phone.

The phone smashed into the wall and busted apart.

The pieces were stomped and pushed by shuffling feet and rolling travel bags.

The mother jogged behind the twins, yelling, "Stevie! Larry! Stop!"

Stevie jumped up and dashed farther into the airport with Larry and Mom in hot pursuit.

By the time my well-meaning co-travelers hauled me off the floor, the phone's pieces were nowhere to be found. They had probably been kicked around and trampled on and who knew what else.

I dusted myself off and righted my luggage and paid for my coffee and moved to the side of the counter out of the melee.

I stretched all my limbs and examined myself for bleeding, but saw none. There would be bruises, especially on my hip where I'd landed on that hard suitcase wheel. But bruises weren't lethal.

Briefly, I thought about how the Boss had learned Summer was on her way to Fort Bird and who else knew her plans. And then I shrugged and pulled out my personal phone and sent him a text. "Phone destroyed." He'd know what to do.

CHAPTER TWO

Friday, November 19
11:43 AM
Fort Bird, North Carolina

COLONEL EUNICE SUMMER, RECENTLY promoted
Commanding Officer of the Army's 110th Special Investigations
Unit, had been married to the Army her whole life. Twenty-five
years of her service was dedicated to investigating crimes and
assuring that punishment was swiftly delivered.

Which was how she'd met Jack Reacher. The Boss sent me
to interview her while my partner, Carlos Gaspar, was
temporarily occupied in Miami.

Before and after her call, my plan was the same. A quick trip
to Fort Bird to learn whatever the Boss believed Summer knew
and get out of the mountains ahead of the coming ice storm.

For the first time in eighteen days, I'd chosen the four-wheel
drive rental vehicle suited to my size and mission. I flipped on
the headlights and windshield wipers, and ran the defrosters full
blast. I made slow progress through the dreary weather from the

Charlotte airport onward, which churned my stomach at the two-antacid level.

I hadn't called Summer after the lost phone because I'd already told her I'd meet her at Fort Bird. Nor did I want to risk any security breaches from my personal phone.

The GPS sent me north on the Interstate and directed me to exit behind a line of assorted vehicles before I reached New Haven.

The sign at the entrance said:

FORT BIRD

HOME OF THE AIRBORNE

AND

SPECIAL OPERATIONS FORCES

I followed a trail of vehicles until it backed up at the main gate. The digital clock on the SUV's dashboard said I was fifteen minutes behind schedule.

I reached into my pocket for another antacid and placed it under my tongue.

Being late is about the worst thing an FBI Special Agent can be, in my book. Tardiness says, "I'm more important than you are. I have no respect for your time." Never a good way to start an interview when what I needed was a lot of cooperation from any witness, and especially a powerful one like Colonel Summer.

Gaspar had been behind the wheel, driving us around as my number two, from the outset of our off-the-books assignment. My driving skills were rusty, so I'd been too cautious on the road. That's why I was late and popping antacids.

As it turned out, my being on time would have made no difference at all.

When it was my turn to be logged in, I pulled up to the sentry station and lowered my window to talk to the soldier inside. A frigid breeze blew cold rain in my face.

"FBI Special Agent Kim Otto," I told the soldier in the booth. "I have an appointment with Colonel Summer."

"Colonel Summer is not posted here at Fort Bird, Ma'am."

I nodded. "She's driving down from Rock Creek."

"She hasn't arrived since I came on duty at zero-nine-thirty." He found my name on the visitors list. Three minutes for paperwork and he gave me a pass and waved me through.

I kept my gun. Army personnel weren't allowed to carry personal weapons on base, but I'm FBI. Which normally wouldn't grant me any kind of special treatment, but the Boss had worked his magic on this issue before I arrived.

I followed signs to the visitor parking lot in front of the low block building that housed Fort Bird's Military Police. I used my personal phone to dial the number I'd memorized from Summer's earlier call. The phone rang several times and went to voicemail. I kept the message cryptic, just in case: "Otto here. I've arrived. I'll wait for you inside the XO's office."

I slipped the transmission into park, turned off all the SUV's dials and buttons, scooped up my phone and my briefcase and hurried inside where it felt good to be warmed by central heat again.

A sergeant seated behind a spotlessly clean and empty desk greeted me with slightly surly disinterest. Maybe he didn't want the FBI on his turf or something.

Church, according to the nametape on his uniform located about where a pocket for cigarettes could have been when my dad was in the Army. He stammered slightly when he said Colonel Summer was running late. My stomach settled a bit.

The sentry had been right. At least I'd arrived before she did.

Colonel Eunice Summer was a lead. A solid lead. And she had been ordered to answer my questions by none other than the Army Chief of Staff. A refreshing change.

I'd planned to ask Summer every question on my three-page list, to squeeze every ounce of information from her until she was drier than a well-juiced lemon. If I was really lucky, she might still have a phone number for Reacher. Even a long-outdated last known address would be the camel's nose under the tent. A place to start.

No matter what, when I left here I'd vowed to have learned *something* about Jack Reacher that would lead me in a straight line right to the end of this assignment.

Sitting there in the warm room, drinking coffee, waiting for Summer, I let myself believe I was on the right side and success was finally headed my way.

CHAPTER THREE

A SLIGHT TOUCH ON MY shoulder and a deeply sexy male voice pulled me from concentration like being gently awakened from an engrossing dream. "Is everything satisfactory, Agent Otto?"

The effect of the man's sudden physical manifestation, however, was anything but gentle. More like an excruciating five-second Taser shock to my system that seemed to temporarily short-out my faculty of speech. After blinking like an idiot for several dumb seconds, I managed to focus on the MP with the mega-watt smile standing directly in front of me. A man who could only be described as dangerously hot.

The realization was not welcome.

I'm not indifferent to men. I've been surrounded by men my whole life. I have three brothers. I went to law school and business school. I work in the mostly male FBI as a field agent. I'd even been married to a man once, a long time ago.

But I *never* mixed business with pleasure.

And I don't trust handsome men. Intelligence, honor,

compassion, integrity and most of all, reliability. Those are my aphrodisiacs now.

Yet there he was, definitely impressive as hell. Green eyes. Black hair. Dark skin. Tall enough. And the voice. A melodious baritone like a radio personality or maybe the old-fashioned crooners my grandmother enjoyed. Until now, I hadn't fully appreciated their appeal.

He squeezed my shoulder and bent his knees to place his gaze at my eye level. "Agent Otto, are you all right?"

"Yes. Of course." I jerked my head quickly and blinked and cleared my throat. "Sorry."

He released his grip on my shoulder and pushed himself upright. He moved aside to give me room to stand and extend my right hand. His handshake was appropriately firm and brief, no more, no less.

"Major Anthony Clifton. Tony to my friends." He had flashed the mega-watt smile again before he got down to business. "I'm the duty officer today. I'm sorry I wasn't here to meet you. Sergeant Church tells me you've been waiting awhile. I've been briefed on your mission. Maybe I can help you until Colonel Summer arrives."

He led the way into a strictly utilitarian office decorated in Army-shabby. Probably ten by twelve. Smallish desk, two visitor chairs, a phone and a computer on the desk, a small window that overlooked a side yard. There was nothing remotely personal or comfortable anywhere in the room, which made me wonder how long Clifton had occupied it—and whether it had looked exactly the same when Reacher worked here.

He waved me to the chair closest to the window and settled himself in the desk chair. Sergeant Church brought three mugs of steaming black coffee and placed them on the desk and closed the door on his way out.

"I know the Army's short on manpower these days," I said, glad to hear that my voice worked, "but why is a sergeant on desk duty and serving coffee? Seems like high-priced talent for a reception job."

"Our clerk's position was eliminated. Church is having a problem with his social life or something. He's been late for duty two days in a row, yesterday and today." Clifton shrugged. "The XO figured he could do with some mild discipline."

"How's he taking that?" He'd been a little surly to me when I first arrived, which I'd thought at the time was due to the FBI invading the Military Police's turf. But maybe he was pissed off at his situation.

Clifton grinned. "He's taking it about as well as you would, I suspect."

"Aren't you the XO? I didn't take you for such a hard-ass."

"You've only just met me." He flashed the mega-watter again. "Wait until you get to know me better."

I frowned. Was he *flirting* with me? Whatever charm he'd exuded in the first five minutes had most definitely worn off. I drank my coffee and offered no witty banter.

A quick rap rattled the door before it opened and a middle-aged woman, maybe about forty-five, stepped inside. She was all bone and sinew, hard, not an ounce of fat on her. Dressed in jeans, work boots, and a leather bomber jacket, her posture said she'd been Army once. Through and through.

She glanced my way before she pulled off her leather gloves and stuffed them into the back pocket of her jeans. She grabbed one of the coffee mugs, sniffed appreciatively, and shook hands with Clifton.

She raised her cup. "I really do miss Army coffee. Best in the world, no question."

He raised his own mug in a silent toast and sipped with her before he nodded in my direction. "Sergeant Major Madeline Jones, this is FBI Special Agent Kim Otto."

"Sergeant Major Madeline Jones, *retired*," she corrected him. Her accent was a thick drawl, so it sounded like re-tarrrrred. Her hand was calloused and her grip was as tough as the rest of her. "My pleasure, Agent Otto."

"Good to meet you as well," I replied, baffled by her presence but unwilling to ask about it just yet.

Jones settled into the second visitor chair, the one closest to the door. She smelled piney like she'd been outside in the woods for a couple of hours. Her hair was short and it looked like she'd cut it herself with nail scissors. She'd recently been wearing a hat, too, which didn't help the hairstyle any.

She sipped her coffee and waited to hear why she'd been invited, probably. Me, too.

Clifton said, "Sergeant Major Jones was on active duty here at Bird from 1985 until, what, 2010?"

Jones nodded, sipped again. She rested the side of her right boot on her left knee. The boots had thick-tread soles that shed most of the mud she'd been clomping around in, but held onto wet dirt and leaves. As the debris dried, she'd be leaving a trail even a blind squirrel could follow.

"Jones was a sergeant when Major Reacher was briefly the XO, meaning executive officer to the Provost Marshal, at the tail end of 1989, early 1990. Jones also reported to Colonel Summer, who was an MP Lieutenant back then." Clifton leaned both forearms on the desk and held the warm coffee mug between his palms, letting his gaze encompass both of us sitting across from him. "Back then, the Berlin Wall was coming down, the Cold War ending," he said as if he'd actually been in charge all those years ago. "The whole world was changing, inside the Army and out."

"Long time ago and lots of changes since then." Jones pursed her lips and moved them around as if she were swishing coffee mouthwash, then turned to me. "I'm glad to help you if I can, Agent Otto. I'm not right sure what I can offer, though. I wasn't a member of the 110th like Major Reacher was. I worked MP here at Bird and pretty closely with Major Reacher, but only for a couple of weeks. Until Colonel Summer called me about your background check, I hadn't heard anything about Major Reacher in two decades, at least."

My stomach clenched. Was there anyone Colonel Summer *hadn't* mentioned my assignment to?

"Maybe we can save a little time, then," I said. "What did Colonel Summer already tell you about the reason for my visit?"

The Army is notoriously protective of its own, particularly when the facts might tarnish the reputation of the top brass. I didn't expect to get much from a careerist like Jones, retired or not. Anyway, she had barely known Reacher. How much information could she possibly have?

Jones adopted a clipped style, probably a habit formed during three decades of making verbal law enforcement reports. "Colonel Summer said Major Reacher is being considered for a high-level classified assignment and the FBI is investigating his fitness for the job."

She'd succinctly stated my cover story well enough. I nodded. "Special Personnel Task Force. We're conducting a background check on Jack Reacher. Bringing his files up to date."

Jones mirrored my nod as if she was interrogating a suspect. "I told Colonel Summer I wouldn't recommend Reacher for any assignment. Maybe he's changed since 1990, but back then he was way too volatile for my liking."

My heart had skipped a beat before it settled into a little bit faster rhythm. "What do you mean?"

She swigged her coffee, cupped her left hand around her ankle and leaned back in the chair to look me full in the eye. "He was only posted here a few days. In that short time, he managed to piss off just about everybody he came in contact with. His behavior got him busted back to Captain." Her tone was as hard now as everything else about her. "What more can you possibly need to know?"

What I really wanted to know was what Reacher had done to piss *her* off. Whatever it was, Jones had been holding onto her grudge for a very long time. The Army had been her life and probably her lifeline, judging from the look of her. The grudge must have been personal, too, based on her bitterness. More than general protectiveness of the Army by a retired MP, for sure. But maybe she was protective of her old unit and resentful that Reacher had sullied it, somehow. Could have been that.

At least on the surface, though, that didn't make sense. Reacher was a rising star back then. He'd stayed in the Army another seven years after he was demoted to Captain in 1990 and he got promoted back to Major again pretty quickly. He couldn't have done anything too terrible here at Bird.

Unfortunately. If he *had* committed a serious enough crime, he'd be living at Leavenworth now where I could easily find him and wrap up my assignment and get back to my life later this afternoon.

"Can you give me a specific example?"

"Like what?" She swigged again.

"I need to explain your answer to my boss." She narrowed her eyes at that and said nothing. I said, "Was he a gambler? A hot head? Anger issues? Did he screw up a case? What exactly was the problem?"

Jones cocked her head as if she was deciphering the question and working out exactly how to frame her answer. "This is a military police unit, Agent Otto. Like you, we are used to dealing with criminal behavior of all stripes. But we keep it in-house. We don't take our dirty laundry outside."

"And you're saying Reacher did that? That's a complaint I haven't heard about him before." I stalled a couple of beats to suggest that I was seriously considering her input. She was right about the coffee, at least. It *was* great. "If anything, I've repeatedly heard the opposite—that he had a tendency to handle things in his own way when he should have deferred to others."

"Like I said, maybe he's changed. Some people do. He was arrogant, disrespectful and downright insubordinate back then. A loner who lived by his own rules. He didn't make many friends while he was here, that's for damn sure." She drained the coffee cup and stood. "I've gotta run. My nephew is waiting for me at the football field. All I can say is, if I was looking for a likable guy to handle an important job as a member of a good team, I'd keep looking. You can do better."

"I'm required to bring his file up to date, though. Eventually, I'll have to interview him." I stood to shake her hand again and met her steady gaze. "Do you know anybody who might still keep in touch with Reacher?"

"Army personnel are transient for the most part. The only reason I turned down promotions to stay here all these years is that my whole family lives in this area and I had my son. He was a baby back when Major Reacher was here. I didn't have the luxury of taking off whenever I felt like it." Jones was already half out the door, but she turned back. "Colonel Summer is your best bet. She's a bulldog. Never gives up. And probably the only one still around here who knew much about Reacher. He also had some buddies in his unit, the 110th. They were spread out all over the place, though. I think I heard there's only a couple of them still alive, but they'd still be worth a try, maybe."

She flashed a little wave and stepped across the threshold, pulling the door closed behind her. Major Clifton cleared his throat, drawing my gaze from the door.

"She always was as hard as woodpecker lips." He shook his head and smiled in a way that revealed the straight white teeth in a quick flash. "I'm a popular guy, but she never liked me, either."

"Any idea what happened between her and Reacher?" Until now, I hadn't met even one woman who was willing to say a bad word of any kind about Reacher. Yet Jones radiated palpable animosity toward him after no contact with the man for almost twenty years. The contrast was curious at the very least. How could Reacher have angered her so deeply during their brief period of contact? Seemed like a stretch for any normal human.

"No clue. Sorry." He picked up the coffee cups and moved through the door behind Jones. "I'll get us a refill. Be right back."

Not just a pretty face after all. Clifton was useful, too. At least he didn't ask me to get coffee, which was a step in the right direction.

CHAPTER FOUR

A ROUTINE BACKGROUND CHECK of the type I was
allegedly performing on this assignment always began with an
existing file. Reacher's file was thin. Too thin. It had obviously
been sanitized and someone on the inside of the FBI and
Homeland Security and maybe the Army and probably a few
other three-letter agencies was making sure it stayed that
way.

Every search I'd tried to conduct had been blocked by
someone much higher up the food chain. I had no leverage to
improve the situation. Which was how I came to be sitting here
in Fort Bird, North Carolina, discussing ancient history on a
nasty November morning.

According to the few records I'd been able to unearth, in
January 1990, Jack Reacher suffered two serious blows. The
strong left hook to the jaw was delivered to his profession. The
straight right to the gut was personal. Either could have buckled
even a man of Reacher's size and strength, and both hits had
indeed caused significant damage.

Sergeant Major Jones was carrying a grudge against

Reacher, but Reacher probably toted a few against Fort Bird and its personnel, too. Add a few thousand soldiers trained as weapons and combat experts and that volatile combination was bound to lead to trouble.

While Clifton was gone, I ran quickly through the information the Boss had provided. Everything had been looking good for Reacher on December 28, 1989. He was large and in charge. Thirty years old. Out of West Point for more than six years. One of the Army's best.

Already a Major and on his way up in the elite 110 Special Investigative Unit. The way things were going, Reacher might have been the commanding officer of the 110th in due course, instead of Summer. Any man basking in those circumstances would have believed the world was his oyster. He'd have been right.

Then everything changed.

He'd been transferred from a high-profile assignment without notice the next day.

Posted to sleepy Fort Bird, North Carolina, where nothing exciting ever happened.

Except it did, to Reacher: Twenty days later, he was demoted to Captain and shipped out to Panama.

And at the same time his career was falling apart, Reacher's mother died.

Then-Lieutenant Eunice Summer had been right next to Reacher the whole time. Whatever happened during those three weeks catapulted her career even as it blew Reacher's a giant leap backward.

Summer might have been responsible for Reacher's troubles, or the beneficiary of his misfortune. Either way, she had firsthand experience with Reacher that no one I'd met so far was willing to talk about. Experience that might just lead me where I needed to go.

I was close. Very close. Closer than I'd been since that 4:00 a.m. phone call from the Boss pulled me out of my warm bed in Detroit eighteen days ago and sent me chasing after a ghost who, I'd believed until recently, might not even exist anymore.

As Jones said, my cover assignment is to build the Reacher file for some top secret project and keep everything under the radar. I'm number one. Gaspar, my number two, was temporarily out of touch.

I'd quickly discovered that the Boss was hunting Reacher and using me like a submarine uses sonar. I still didn't know why. But I would.

This was the Army. There should be records and files and witnesses in triplicate to everything Reacher did here at Bird, at the very least. All I had to do was find them.

Major Clifton returned with two mugs full of coffee. He kicked the door closed with his heel, handed me one of the mugs, and returned to his seat behind the desk with the second mug.

I watched him carefully this time, trying to peer beyond his handsome façade. Colonel Summer knew what I wanted and she'd been ordered to give it to me, she said. She wouldn't have disobeyed a direct order from that high up. She'd have saluted and prepared. She'd been on her way to do as she'd been told when she called me from her car.

Summer might have asked someone to gather information to refresh her memory for our meeting. That someone was probably seated directly across the desk from me right now. "Major Clifton—"

"Tony." Out flashed the blinding dazzler, his go-to weapon of choice, perhaps his all-purpose shield.

I nodded. "Did Colonel Summer brief you on my mission here today?"

"She said you were interested in a former executive officer who served briefly here at Bird back in 1990 when I was still in junior high school." He leaned back in the chair and rested his coffee on the battered wooden chair arm.

"You are the executive officer here now, though. You hold the job Reacher held back then. Right?"

"I am and I do."

"Did you pull the files on whatever cases Major Reacher was handling at the time? You must have. Otherwise, you wouldn't have known that Sergeant Major Jones was also active duty during Reacher's brief stint here."

He shook his head. "Jones spent her whole career here. It was a safe bet that she worked with Reacher. No file review necessary."

"But you did pull the files." I was guessing, but that's what any XO worth his salt would have done. "And?"

"And what?"

"What was the big case about? And how did Reacher screw it up?"

"What makes you think he screwed up a big case?"

"Something got him demoted to Captain and sent to Panama after less than three weeks here. I'm guessing that something was related to his work while he was here. Are you telling me it wasn't?"

He didn't squirm or blush or even blink, but I sensed he was uncomfortable with the questions and probably with the answers as well. "Actually," he said, "I'm not telling you anything at all. Colonel Summer's orders were very clear. She'll handle this interview herself."

"That would be great. If she were present. But she isn't. Which means the job falls to you, doesn't it?"

"Have you ever been in the Army, Agent Otto?"

I shook my head.

"You don't get to be a major in the U.S. Army by disobeying orders from a superior officer, especially one who is directly in your chain of command." He took a breath, paused, and seemed to make up his mind about something. "In fact, that's the sort of thing that can get you busted back to Captain and sent off to the front of the fighting pretty quickly. Probably take less than three weeks, start to finish."

I nodded again, wondering why he was so reluctant to directly address Reacher's old story. "What other kinds of things can get an officer demoted and transferred like that?"

"Conduct unbecoming would do it. Civilian complaints and officer complaints of a significant nature. Unauthorized absence. Away without leave. Misuse of resources." He listed them slowly as if he had to think about the options, which I was pretty sure he did not. I had the clear impression that these particular offenses came straight out of the facts in Reacher's old case files.

He hesitated a moment and leveled his gaze my way. "This is the Army. There's a long list of don'ts that can get a guy in big trouble pretty fast."

I considered each option he'd offered.

If Reacher had done all that, Jones was right. He was the farthest thing from a team player.

Crazy thing was, busting him back and sending him out of here was a puny slap on the wrist that Reacher would have barely noticed.

CHAPTER FIVE

THE DESK PHONE RANG and Major Clifton answered. He listened for less than a minute, said "Thank you," and hung up.

"The sergeant says Colonel Summer has not arrived and right now she's unreachable." He frowned and tapped his forefinger on the desktop. "It's not unusual for us to get called out without notice like that, but I'm sorry you've come all this way for nothing."

How convenient. And no real surprise, either. Not just because that had so often been how the cards had fallen throughout my investigation into Reacher. Something happened here back in 1990 and it had been buried for twenty years. The Army wouldn't want to open that old can of worms, no matter how cooperative they appeared.

"Happens to me all the time, too." I stood and extended my hand to Major Clifton. "I'll leave a voice mail for Colonel Summer and I'm sure she'll call me when she can."

Another dead end. I was annoyed, but not shocked. Reacher had been off the grid since his honorable discharge. No small feat. Only a clever man with a certain skill set could manage to do that in the modern age. Stood to reason that he'd honed those skills in the Army. I was glad I hadn't pulled Gaspar away from his family and wasted his time as well as mine.

And I wondered why the Boss was pushing these particular hot buttons. He had an ulterior motive. He always did.

Major Clifton dialed the charm factor up to full throttle, now that the Army appeared to have dodged my questions. "In the meantime, is there anyone else here at Bird you'd like to talk with or anything else I can help you find?"

What he meant was that he'd be glad to let me go on a wild goose chase around a base that was as large as Detroit, knowing I'd find nothing of value. I cocked my head so he'd know I was considering the offer.

And I was. Summer had been Reacher's subordinate officer at a time when critical events occurred in Reacher's life. Pressure points. The type that shaped a man, pushed him to make tough choices, revealed his character or changed it, for better or worse.

Someone besides Summer knew what had happened. I could find witnesses, uncover facts, do my job. If everyone would get out of my way. So I deflected. "I have a list of people to interview off the base, but if I hear of anyone back here who might be of interest, it's good to know I'll find the door open."

He frowned but said nothing.

Which probably meant I could look until Hell froze over and I wouldn't find a scrap of paper or a single person at Fort Bird who would tell me anything. Whatever had happened was sensitive and buried too deep. Jones was right, too. Army bases were filled with transients. Most of the soldiers here now hadn't been here two years ago, let alone two decades ago.

Major Clifton walked with me to the front door and

continued along outside, where the November wind sliced through my lightweight suit. I had been in Florida yesterday, where sunshine and temperatures in the 80s had warmed my blood too much. Cold, gusty wind and rain were far from my favorite combination, but it was normal for the season and to be expected. Worse was coming before the mountain weather improved in the spring.

"Look," Major Clifton said, "let me buy you some lunch at least. We can go over to the Officers Club. You've got a long drive to wherever you're going." Now that he'd mentioned lunch, my stomach growled like one of Pavlov's dogs. He delivered the closer: "And who knows, maybe Colonel Summer will get here by the time we've finished."

Maybe Summer had blown me off. Maybe she'd never intended to follow her orders. What did I really know about her? Or maybe her orders were delivered with a wink and a nod. Maybe the Army placated the Boss but never had any intention of following through.

I had no answers to any of that, but I was hungry, so I tossed my briefcase into the front seat of my rental and slammed the door. "Let's go."

Clifton flashed that smile again, which probably worked to get him anything he wanted from most women. Truth be told, the impact wasn't lost on me, either, as much as I wished otherwise.

I hugged my arms around my thin blazer and put my head down against the wind as we walked. Within a dozen steps, the rain became sleet. It pelted my exposed skin like tiny ice needles that melted after contact, leaving only the damage to prove they'd existed.

"Driving on the mountain roads will be treacherous when you leave here," Major Clifton bent his head to make sure his voice carried. "We'll have snow on top of this ice before midnight. You'll want to be very careful and stick to the well-traveled highways as much as possible."

We reached our destination after five minutes of brisk walking, but I was chilled to the bone and my wool suit had absorbed enough icy rain to weigh me down. Inside, the Officers Club was warm and dry. Logs crackled in the fireplace. The place was almost homey.

Most of the tables were already full of officers who had no interest in venturing off base. They were all dressed in what the Army calls ACUs, or Army Combat Uniforms, the standard uniform worn daily on base. ACUs replaced the old BDUs, or Battle Dress Uniforms, that were worn during Reacher's time.

Everything was an acronym around the Army and I often felt like I needed an interpreter. Maybe there was an app for that. I made a mental note to check.

Several officers exchanged brief pleasantries with Major Clifton as we passed through the room. He introduced me to a few. Colonel James Artem, Major Sebastian Rochester, even a General Declan Maunder. Clifton seemed well-regarded by all.

Two female officers, Lieutenants Betty Farish Johnston and Lynne Graham, made a point of engaging him in a longer conversation than was necessary. He appreciated the attention a bit too much, which helped to squelch his appeal for me. My ex had been a little too popular with women. It was a trait I never appreciated.

It didn't take long to choose what turned out to be surprisingly good food from the lunch buffet. Along with a big mug full of that great coffee.

Clifton steered me to an empty table in the back where we could talk quietly without interruption, which I thought was a little curious under the circumstances. He'd already made an elaborate point of pretending he didn't know anything and couldn't tell me what he did know. Why did we need privacy? Unless he was simply on the prowl. In which case he had plenty of willing participants already.

I organized my lunch from the tray to the table while he led the first ten minutes of our conversation. Irrelevant small talk of the kind I'm not good at and never remember afterward.

And then he got to the point. "Listen. I never met Jack Reacher. That was before my time."

I nodded. "How old are you? Thirty-five? Thirty-six?"

"Pretty good guess. I'm thirty-five." He grinned. "How old are you?"

Once I'd begun to eat, I realized how hungry I was. "Irrelevant. This chowder is excellent, though. Hearty and hot."

"Indulge me." When I looked up from my chowder, his eyes were laser-focused on me, which made me wary. I'm not that interesting, not even to my parents.

"Thirty-two," I said. "The perfect age. Or so my mother says."

"Now I'm feeling too old." He cocked his head. He hadn't touched his food. "Did your mother give you a reason for choosing thirty-two as the perfect age?"

He was listening, paying attention, maybe even interested. He wasn't totally self-absorbed. Maybe this guy was more than a pretty face after all. Maybe. But not likely. Men as attractive as he was usually don't bother developing their other talents. They don't need to. The rest of us have to try harder.

What was his motive?

"My mother is Vietnamese-American." I shrugged, spooning the chowder. "She always thinks everything is simultaneously perfect and not perfect. Next year, thirty-three will be the perfect age."

He laughed. His laugh was as deep and warm as his voice. The kind of voice that would make you feel cozy and protected in the middle of the night. A dangerous voice. A woman could be enticed to rely on a voice like that.

Some women. Not this one. "Now that you know everything there is to know about my mother, tell me why you invited me to lunch."

"I was hungry." He still had not touched his food. "I figured you probably were, too. That's all."

"I *was* hungry." I finished the last bit of my chowder to prove it. "But that's not why you asked me to lunch, or why I accepted."

"No?" His left eyebrow arched while the right one didn't move a smidge. Then he reversed the process.

Seriously? Ambidextrous eyebrows?

"I accepted your invitation," I said, "because I want you to tell me more about Colonel Summer. Jones said she's a bulldog. Summer told me she was in the middle of a corruption investigation now. I imagine the bulldog personality helps with work like that. What's the most successful approach for me to take with her to find out everything she knows about Reacher?"

He took a deep breath and squared his shoulders. There he went: He seemed reticent again all of a sudden.

He said, "I asked you to lunch because I might be able to help you."

CHAPTER SIX

"I COULD CERTAINLY USE the help," I said, wondering what he could possibly know that would be of use to me.

"When I was at West Point, Reacher was long gone. I only knew him by reputation." He hesitated a couple of beats. "But my brother knew him."

"Your brother?" I blinked, recalibrating swiftly.

"I had two brothers." He held up two fingers. "Both older and both also at West Point. Frank was in Jack Reacher's class."

The rest of my food instantly lost its appeal and my pulse quickened. An actual witness. "Can I talk to him? Has he kept in touch with Reacher at all?"

"No." He lowered his gaze briefly, cleared his throat and returned a steady stare. "Frank was killed in Desert Storm."

"I'm sorry." I was also confused.

He nodded. "Stories about Jack Reacher are the stuff of legend, though. There are lots of tough guys at West Point and in the Army. We've got a lot of them here on base. Reacher's reputation was different."

"How so?"

"He wasn't well liked or popular. But he was respected."

"Feared, you mean?"

He shrugged. "It's a fine line sometimes. Word was, he never put up with any kind of bullshit. Even from superior officers. Had a very low tolerance level for crap coming his way. And because he was so huge, people didn't mess with him and live to tell about it, if you know what I mean." He paused. Cleared his throat again. "But my older brother, Matt, was at West Point with *Joe* Reacher."

Reluctant to rush into another faux pas, I said nothing.

"For another few days until he reports for new orders, that brother, Major General Matthew Clifton, is the Commander of the First Team." I must have looked as clueless as I surely felt because he explained. "The 1st Cavalry Division in Fort Herald, Texas."

I shook my head. Of course, I'd heard of the 1st Cavalry. But what I knew had been gleaned mostly from the movie *Apocalypse Now*, which loosely followed the 1st Cavalry Division during the Viet Nam war. I'd always been interested in the Viet Nam conflict because my parents met and fell in love when Dad was serving in the Army there.

"One of the most decorated divisions of the Army." Major Clifton leaned in and lowered his voice. "If you give me your word that I can trust you to keep this confidential, I will ask Matt your questions. He may or may not have answers. But he liked and respected Joe Reacher immensely. They were very close at West Point and for quite a while afterward. Up until Joe died."

I remained silent. I'd learned a few facts about Joe Reacher's death early in my assignment. He'd died in the line of duty in a small Georgia town, not long after Jack Reacher left the Army fifteen years ago.

"In our business, we see a lot of death. We've lost friends and family many times over." His gaze seemed to be asking for my consent, but consent to what? "Joe Reacher was a special friend to Matt and I know he would want to help Joe's brother."

Only then did Major Clifton tuck into his meal, giving me time to work things out while he ate.

His implied question was tricky. If General Matthew Clifton told me whatever he knew about Joe Reacher, would that information help Joe's brother, Jack?

The truth was, I had no idea why the Boss tasked us with building a file on Jack Reacher or what he would do with the data we uncovered. The job Reacher was being considered for was classified and above my clearance level.

But there was a lot that was hinky about the whole business.

The Boss wanted to find Jack Reacher. And he usually sent us to places he felt Reacher was likely to show up. He believed the key to finding Reacher lay with his old contacts. That was really all I knew for sure. For a normal human, that would be a good strategy, too. We'd exploited it many times in routine FBI investigations.

What I suspected, but couldn't prove, was that the Boss was illegally monitoring Reacher's old contacts. When they were either already or about to be enmeshed in serious trouble and the Boss thought Reacher might show up, he sent Gaspar and me into the middle of the situation.

If that's what he was doing, the Boss was breaking every rule there was. He likely believed that if we got a good result, breaking the rules might not matter.

Based on what I'd learned so far, that seemed to be Reacher's philosophy, too. The two of them were well-matched that way.

On the flip side, I didn't know whether Reacher was actively hiding or simply hadn't been located yet. Big difference. The behavior of everyone we'd met who had actually known Reacher was wary and suspicious, at best. Which strongly suggested that Reacher had good reason to hide.

Nothing about my off-the-books assignment was normal or routine or even explainable. I'd been told to stay under the radar. Not undercover, but pretty damn close. I'd been given permission to share a sanitized version of my orders when required, but nothing more.

And General Clifton would have questions, no doubt. Questions I couldn't answer.

Short story long, even if I wanted to tell Major Tony Clifton and his brother all about my assignment, I'd been ordered not to do so. Violating orders wasn't a healthy way to get ahead in the FBI. And I couldn't promise anything about what the Boss would do or not do with the information I managed to acquire, anyway.

So the tough question was whether I would volunteer more to Tony Clifton now and tell him what was really going on, against my orders, or not. I'd ignored the Boss before and I didn't have a philosophical problem with doing so when the situation called for it.

But this time, the answer was no. For two reasons.

The first was my number two, Gaspar. I was the lead agent on this case so it was my call to make, but I couldn't put his career on the line without asking him, at the very least. He needed this job and he'd made it plain he would do whatever was required to stay employed. He had four kids and another due any minute and a wife to support and twenty years to go before he retired. He was disabled and this was the only job he could get.

Gaspar's career was not mine to risk. Simple as that.

The second thing was, I intended to be the director of the FBI someday. The road to that particular brass ring was long and winding. The Boss could help me or he could make damn sure I never reached my destination.

So far, he'd been in my corner. Mostly.

The Boss had already made the call, contacting General Clifton again would be a waste of time. If he hadn't called, he wouldn't appreciate me doing so unless I could produce something tangible. At the moment, I had no clue how I could make that happen.

I pushed my plate away, crossed my ankles and sat more comfortably with my coffee. The icy rain pelted harder against the windows and I had no real desire to rush. What I did have was a rare chance to get some straight answers, even though the answers were old.

"Did you ever meet Joe Reacher?"

Major Clifton nodded. "A few times. I was just a kid when Matt brought him home for a weekend or two. Joe's parents were posted overseas and Jack was with them, so Joe was on his own for a couple of years before Jack entered West Point."

"What was Joe like?"

"Big. Tall. Wide. As a kid, I thought he was a giant. Studious, I guess you'd say. More than a little exacting sometimes." He grinned and tore off a piece of bread to sop up the last of his chowder. "Joe didn't have a middle name, but he joked that if he had, it would have been Joe Pedantic Reacher."

We both laughed at that. "That's quite a concept for a kid to remember."

"I'll never forget this." Major Clifton nodded slowly, smiling still. "Joe was teaching me to play chess. I might have been oh, I don't know, eight or so at the time. I played pretty well for an eight-year-old. But nowhere near as good as Joe. He wanted me to learn some complicated opening move and I just couldn't get it. He wouldn't give up, though. He said he taught Jack to play chess and he knew he could teach me, too. He played with me for hours that weekend. It was a lot of attention for a boy to get from one of his big brother's buddies."

I filed away the chess player comment to consider later. Reacher as a chess master made sense. The Boss was playing an elaborate game with Reacher and I believed Reacher knew it and was making his own countermoves.

Something in Clifton's tone led me to ask, "Not altogether welcome attention from Joe, sounds like."

"At the time, I think I just wanted to play baseball with my friends." He finished his meal and pushed his plate away. "In retrospect, I see how extraordinary it was for Joe to do that. There were probably other things he would rather have been doing, too."

"He sounds like a decent guy."

"He really was. I thought so then and I still do. There was a girl in our neighborhood that he liked. What was her name? Linda? Lauren? Lilly?" He closed his eyes a moment as if he might recall her name if he could visualize her. He shook his head. "Sorry. I can't remember. But she was old man Browning's girl. We called him 'old man,' but he was probably not more than forty-five at the time. Anyway, he didn't like Joe at all."

"Why not?"

He shrugged. "He wouldn't have liked any boy trying to date his daughter. And she—well, she was just—I don't know. Crazy, my brother said. Not a mental case, but—a piece of work. You know what I mean?"

I nodded, thinking about my sister at that age. Certainly

headstrong. Definitely crazy about boys. There for a while it seemed she might cause my dad to stroke out with her foolishness. "So what happened?"

"Well, there was a long weekend break. Joe came home with Matt and she was there and—I don't know." He shrugged again. "I was a kid. But I guess they eloped or something."

"Eloped?" I hadn't seen that one coming. "Joe Reacher and this girl got married?"

"Yeah, I guess so. Though they kept it to themselves for a while. She came back home and Joe went back to school. Nobody seemed to notice." He grinned again. "Old man Browning was off the charts when he found out a few weeks later. He came over with a baseball bat, threatening to beat Joe with it. Fortunately for all of us, Joe wasn't there."

"What happened to the girl?"

"I guess they must have divorced or maybe they never really got married. I don't know. She came home, but Joe never did come back to our house after Matt told him about the baseball bat." He drained his coffee mug and placed it on the table.

I'd been so engrossed in Joe Reacher's story that I hadn't seen Sergeant Church approach. He startled me when he spoke. "M-M-Major Clifton? The Provost Marshal requests a 10-19 im-mm-mediately."

A 10-19 meant the Provost wanted Clifton to call him. Why couldn't the Army speak the same English as the rest of the country?

Clifton thanked him, and then as if he'd remembered something, asked, "Sergeant Church? Wasn't your dad with the 110th around 1990?"

Church nodded. "Not for long, Sir. The 110th was his last command before he died."

"Ah. Well. Thanks, Sergeant." Church nodded again, and then Clifton got to his feet and beamed that smile down at me. "Will you excuse me, Agent Otto? I'm sorry Colonel Summer couldn't keep your appointment. She could still show up. You're welcome to stay here as long as you like."

"I need to go anyway. I've got a lot to do yet." I stood with them. "I'll most likely get back to you on your offer to help if I may."

Clifton and I shook hands. "You bet. Glad to do it. Anytime."

He walked away with Church, who seemed to limp slightly, which reminded me of Gaspar. I watched their retreating backs for a second before leaving the warmth behind and hustling away through the sleet as quickly as my slipping, sliding leather soles would take me.

I was soaked and shivering again by the time I settled into the rental's driver's seat. The windshield was covered with a thin layer of ice and the wipers were frozen to it. I wasn't about to stand out there scraping the windshield with my credit card and freezing to death. People said you don't catch a cold from being cold, but I've never believed that. I started the engine and blasted the heat and defrosters for a full five minutes before I could move the ice and see well enough to leave the parking lot.

"Now there's a metaphor, Otto. Your entire assignment is iced over and you're stuck in park, aren't you?" A sour grin stole onto my mouth, but no one was there to notice.

CHAPTER SEVEN

I PUSHED THE REVERSE route button on the GPS unit in the rental when I stopped at the exit gate. I returned my visitor's pass and the soldier handed me a sealed manila envelope.

The envelope was unmarked aside from my name printed in all capital letters in the center. It was too flat to contain much of anything. "What's this?"

"I don't know, ma'am. I was instructed to deliver it after you surrendered your pass." He touched the brim of his hat—not a salute exactly, but a friendly gesture. Someone inside the booth said something and he nodded. "Road reports are bad out there, ma'am. You're not going over the mountain, are you? There's been a serious accident and the highway is closed. Better off taking the long way back to the airport, in this weather. You want to arrive in one piece."

"Good to know. Thanks."

Delivering an envelope to me like that was exactly the sort of thing the Boss would do. Not in the mood for his brand of cat-and-mouse, I tossed the envelope onto the passenger seat.

I glanced into the rearview mirror and found a line of

vehicles behind me, waiting to be logged out. I waved, the soldier raised the gate and I rolled slowly away from Fort Bird along the slick pavement.

As I pushed through the gate, I simultaneously pushed another button on the GPS for an alternate route. The distance showing on the screen was about thirty miles off-base to the edge of New Haven, the closest town. Ten miles longer than the newer route due north over the mountain, which the sentry said was closed. That left the old county road, which had been the only road when Reacher was the XO in 1990, as the last northbound option.

When there's only one choice, it's the right choice, as my mother would say.

None of the vehicles passing through the gate turned north behind me. The uneasy feeling that they knew something I didn't about the best way out of here settled in my bones.

Even with the four-wheel drive, my speed never increased above fifteen miles an hour along the county road, although the posted limit was fifty-five. Traffic was light through the North Carolina countryside, but after the third oncoming vehicle had slid across the center line, requiring me to employ evasive maneuvers, I moved as far onto the wide gravel shoulder as possible.

Tension gripped my neck and shoulders as tightly as my hands clawed the steering wheel. My stomach was a churning mess and the delicious chowder lunch threatened to make an encore appearance, but I dared not dart my hand into my pocket to fish out an antacid.

The gray sky darkened as weak November daylight gave up the fight much earlier than expected. My headlights had been on the whole way, but I could barely see twenty feet ahead. Strip malls, scrubby pines, and dormant fields were obscured by fog.

People would be hunched inside on a dismal day like this, log fires burning in fireplaces or, at the very least, electric space heaters blasting. There were sure to be a couple of tragic fires overnight when the cheap heaters failed in various predictable ways.

The GPS showed my SUV steadily consuming the distance to town, but I saw no proof of civilization ahead.

My phone rang and I glanced over to where I'd placed it on the passenger seat on top of the flat manila envelope. The caller ID said *Gaspar*. My fingers had cramped around the steering wheel and refused all efforts to pry them loose until long after the ringing stopped.

The forty-minute drive from Bird devolved into a two-hour ordeal, but the GPS had not lied. Eventually, an intersection with a traffic light and a small green sign marking the New Haven town limits revealed itself.

The sign was a divider between here and there. On this side, nothing but icy fields and fog. On that side, a handful of low commercial buildings clustered in the foggy drizzle near the highway interchange that was the first exit north of Fort Bird on the newer mountain highway. I'd have passed by here on my way down to Raleigh. Summer would have passed on her way from Rock Creek, too.

A huge truck stop was the centerpiece, much newer than whatever had occupied the prime real estate during Reacher's time. A square building with plate glass windows on the top half of the stucco walls anchored the middle of the complex. Inside, the building housed a convenience store, two fast-food chain eateries, and public restrooms with showers. Covered fueling stations flanked three sides of the building and a parking lot out back allowed long-haul eighteen wheelers to stay a few hours, grab a shower and try to nap before the next leg of the journey.

The place was designed for efficient coming and going. Definitely not a vacation destination. Yet, every available parking slot in and around the truck stop was occupied by stymied travelers today.

An easy walk past the truck stop was *The Lucky Bar*, a decades-old cinderblock lounge with no windows. Flashing neon signs on the roof were more than twice as tall as the building. Signs faced both north and southbound lanes so that no weary driver could possibly miss them when traveling in either direction.

Totally Nude Girls. Exotic Dancing. Nude Nude Nude. Girls Girls Girls.

Similar highbrow performances beckoned travelers along the entire Interstate highway system through most of the country. This one looked more prosperous than some. Probably because of its proximity to Fort Bird.

The Lucky Bar's parking lot was as big as a football field. Competition for the lucrative entertainment dollar was plentiful both up and downstream, but every parking space I could see here was jammed three deep and vehicles overflowed onto the grass along the road's shoulders. *The Lucky Bar's* cash registers must have been overflowing with cash, too. Not to mention the garters or whatever exotic dancers used to hold their tips.

Conveniently located directly across the road from the gas station was the corresponding hot-sheets hotel. My home away from home for the night. I'd stay ten hours and be their longest tenant in—well—probably forever.

There are thousands of similar roadside budget hotels all over the country. Reacher had probably stayed in a few of them.

This one was a member of the Grand Lodge chain. Invariably, these havens for the travel-weary are less grand than their monikers. They provide a clean, cheap room, a small continental breakfast buffet, and hot coffee. No mini-bar, no room service, and no entertainment beyond pay-per-view porn on the television and an unread Gideon Bible in the nightstand.

Those roadside hotels fortunate enough to have a strip bar across the street probably make quite a bit more profit. Real estate value is all about location.

The traffic light finally turned green. I pulled the SUV into the New Haven Grand Lodge driveway and parked as close as possible to the front entrance. When I stepped out of the warm cabin, the first thing I noticed was the cold. Temperatures had dropped since I'd left Fort Bird. The drizzle had thickened and chilled into slush that slicked the pavement to ice-rink thickness under my leather-soled shoes. I'd been a lousy ice-skater as a kid and I was no better now. Weak ankles or something, my mother said.

The second thing I noticed was the noise. Rumbling diesel engines from the truck stop underscored everything. Music pulsed from *The Lucky Bar* in a sound wave that might have knocked me over if I'd been standing even ten yards closer.

I shrugged. The next exit north might not have a hotel of any kind. I was cold and tired and hungry here and now. Nothing else to be done but collect my bag, lock the SUV and go inside. And try to do it all without falling on my butt.

A cavernous lobby that normally doubled as the breakfast room was more crowded than a sports bar during playoff season. The weather and the accident that had closed the highway had also stranded dozens of travelers. Those who weren't in the bar or the truck stop had squatted here like tailgaters. Palpable cacophony throbbed and squeezed against me from all sides.

I hoped my room was far enough away from the boisterous lobby crowd. I planned to enjoy a peaceful night and regroup in the morning.

CHAPTER EIGHT

AT THE REGISTRATION DESK, a well-groomed young man who might have been a student at the local community college majoring in hospitality, waved and flashed a blinding smile almost as big as the neon signs on the bar across the street. Probably an effort to communicate despite the deafening noise.

I pushed the telescoping handle down on my bag, lifted it, and elbowed my way through to the reception desk. At least the floor was carpeted. I could finally walk without sliding.

The smiling clerk didn't bother with small talk that I couldn't possibly have heard anyway. He simply held out his hand and I placed a credit card on his palm. He clicked a few keys on his computer, handed me a form to sign, then gave me back my card and two room keys and a map of the hotel. I nodded and elbowed my way through the lobby to the elevator bank.

Local news was playing on the television. I couldn't hear the audio. The screen filled with photos and text banners, all about the storm at first, and then several vehicle crashes, including the one that closed the mountain highway between here and Fort Bird.

A news reporter with a handheld microphone was standing in the foreground. The video playing behind him carried a time stamp reflecting that the video was recorded hours earlier, not too long before I arrived at Fort Bird. The clip was pieced from footage from overhead cameras of some kind. Maybe drones or helicopters.

Bad weather had impacted the quality of the video and the images were hard to see from across the lobby. Flashing lights from five or six police and rescue vehicles were gathered around two tractor-trailer combos, one in front, and one behind what might have been a red subcompact once upon a time. Now the little red car was mangled beyond all recognition. It looked like a crumpled candy wrapper.

An involuntary shudder ran up my back. I'd almost taken that route on the way to Bird earlier in the day. It was a direct Interstate highway from DC to Miami. If I'd flown into Raleigh, I'd have been on that very highway shortly after that crash. But the Boss routed me to Charlotte and the drive north because the flight times were better.

There but for the Grace of God...

Next up on the television was the weather map, which showed the storm moving across the entire central East Coast, confirmed there was zero chance I'd be driving anywhere else tonight. Not that I'd planned to.

The elevator pinged. The doors slid open. A half-dozen revelers fell out. I entered and pressed the button for the third floor. The doors slid closed, but I heard the boisterous crowd through the elevator shaft all the way up.

When I reached the third-floor elevator lobby, the plate glass windows rumbled to the cadence of the diesel trucks and the booming music and rowdy crowd overflowing *The Lucky Bar.*

My room wasn't far down the corridor. From inside room 309, a single window provided a straight sightline to everything from the Grand Lodge to the highway on the west side of the truck stop directly across. The fog and sleet obscured my view but didn't eliminate it entirely.

The Lucky Bar's door was propped open, even in this weather. I couldn't see the crowd inside, but a steady stream of middle-aged road warriors strode in and staggered out. On ordinary nights, the place was probably a favorite social spot for locals and enlisted personnel from Fort Bird, too. If there were any Army in there tonight, their local bar was no longer theirs. Locals were outnumbered tonight by stranded civilians, for sure.

While I watched, three pairs of exotic dancers and their escorts crossed the road toward the Grand Lodge, while two lone women trudged back from the hotel toward *The Lucky Bar*, having evidently lost their customers to ESPN or perhaps unconsciousness now that their transactions had been completed. I rubbed my sore neck with my right hand and counted myself lucky to have a bed tonight that didn't already have a hooker in it.

My room's window glass vibrated to the heavy beat of country music, despite the distance. Soundproofing in this room was non-existent. I wondered how difficult it was to perform exotic dances accompanied by twangy voices, guitars, and fiddle music, whether the dancers were nude or otherwise. Was there such a thing as naked Texas Two-Step or country line dancing?

I turned up the heat in the room and pulled out my phone. Gaspar had left his message more than an hour ago, so I cranked up the volume and listened to that first.

"No baby yet. False alarm. Man, this kid is stubborn. I know what you're thinking: Just like his old man. Well, maybe so.

Either way, the doctors are sending Marie home. I can get away in a few hours. Give me a call when you get this and we'll make a plan."

He sounded exhausted. Baby business or no, he never slept well because of the pain in his right side and right leg. But his disability was a subject we never discussed. As long as he did the job, he was entitled to some privacy.

A new text from the Boss had come in an hour ago while I was white-knuckled on the road. One word: "Status?"

I texted back: "Grounded by NC weather."

He immediately replied: "Drive up. Meet you at National."

He wanted me to drive almost three hundred miles to DC tonight, in this weather? Not a chance. I typed "No," and slipped the phone into my pocket. It was a word he didn't hear often from anyone.

Half a second later my phone vibrated, which I ignored. It was late. I was tired. I'd accomplished nothing today worth reporting and the Boss already knew that because he knew everything. There was no reason to talk to him.

The hotel had no room service, but there was a menu on top of the television for delivery from the fast food joint inside the truck stop. I ordered a vegetarian sub with a two-liter bottle of water. They had beer on the menu and a few cheap domestic wines. I ordered a bottle of cabernet. She repeated my room number and said my delivery would arrive soon.

After that, I unpacked and fired up my laptop, then pressed redial on my phone.

"Took you long enough to call back." Gaspar sounded more exhausted than before, but he was probably hamming it up. He had been at the hospital with Marie most of the day, which meant he'd already managed a dozen catnaps. He was a master at that particular skill. He'd told me one thing he'd learned in the Army was how to sleep anywhere.

"My life is a never-ending party," I assured him. I glanced around the room. It was clean enough and not unreasonably worn. Utilitarian all the way. No mini-bar. Not even a coffee pot. Styrofoam cups wrapped in plastic. I just hoped there were no bed bugs. "Yeah, I'm living in the lap of luxury here. You don't know what you're missing, Zorro."

"Tell me about it, then. Take my mind off everything that's not happening here."

"Still no baby?" I looked at my watch. "How long has Marie been in labor?"

"She wasn't, I guess. The doctors don't seem too worried. I think they went out for a round of golf or something."

Gaspar was a dedicated family man. He was extremely proud of his four daughters, but totally over the moon about the arrival of his first boy. Not that he ever let on, of course. At least, not to me, and definitely not to the Boss.

I quickly filled him in on the non-results of my trip to Fort Bird. Anyone who was listening could hear me, too, but I hadn't learned anything worth protecting.

"Joe Reacher was married once, huh?" he said. "That's a bit of news. Possibly, we could get a lead of some sort from the ex-wife although it was a long time ago. She could know something helpful about Jack Reacher, I guess. Maybe a last known address or the name of a friend who did keep in touch?"

"Since I'm stuck in this hotel room, I'll see if I can track her down. Maybe we can see her tomorrow, depending on where she's living now." I heard three quick raps on the door followed by a female voice announcing the arrival of my gourmet meal. "Be right back."

I tossed the phone on the bed, unbolted the door, and collected the paper bags from a young woman who probably had a side job as a dancer at *The Lucky Bar*. She was about thirty, tall and thin, not particularly pretty. Her makeup had been shoveled on with a trowel. Perhaps her beauty was enhanced by the stage lights around the dancing poles. Her shiny orange raincoat barely reached mid-thigh and, based on the gaping spaces between the coat buttons, she wore nothing underneath but goosebumps.

We transferred paper bags and cash. She snorted, obviously unimpressed by my three-dollar tip on a four-dollar bottle of wine and three-dollar sandwich. She wrapped her fingers around the money, revealing long fingernails covered in thickly sparkling pink glitter. She shoved her hand into her coat pocket and left without saying a word.

When I returned to the phone, Gaspar said, "Hang on."

He was talking to someone else. Something had happened with Marie a few days ago that worried him. But he wouldn't tell me what was going on. It wasn't relevant to our assignment and I didn't like to pry.

The disembodied voices reminded me of the soldier at Fort Bird's exit gate who had handed me the flat manila envelope. I'd set it aside to analyze later and forgotten about it during the harrowing drive. It took me a couple of seconds to find where I'd stuffed it.

Gaspar came back on the line. "Sorry, Boss Lady. I have to run. Anything else we need to deal with right now?"

"This whole area for two hundred miles in either direction is a giant ice slick. I'm in for the night." I held the curious envelope up toward the light. "With any luck, I'll find Joe Reacher's ex-wife and text you an airport nearby wherever she lives for tomorrow. Tell Marie I'm thinking about her."

"10-4," he said, just to be cute. In the Army, 10-4 meant "wrecker requested." For Civilians and police departments, it usually meant "understood" or "confirmed." The FBI doesn't use ten codes because nobody knows what they mean.

Instantly, my phone vibrated again before I had a chance to do anything. Which meant the Boss had been listening. He knew I held the phone in my hand and couldn't very well ignore him again. *What the hell.* "This is FBI Special Agent Kim Otto."

"Lovely room." His voice was quiet, as always. "I can see why you'd rather stay at the luxurious Grand Lodge than follow orders."

Could he actually see me? Right this moment? I thought not. As Gaspar often said, he was the Boss, not God. Nothing about this low-budget room suggested high-tech monitoring devices had been installed, although he'd had plenty of time to set up spy cams before I arrived and make sure I was placed in this room if he'd wanted to.

He also had access to equipment that would permit him to see and hear through the glass from a significant distance. I pulled the heavy drapes closed to block his sightline. I could do nothing about the listening devices if they existed.

"You're right," I said. "Any DC restaurant would be better than my stale sandwich from the truck stop." I shrugged and ran my fingers through my hair. There was no point to fighting this particular battle. I was letting my stubborn nature get the best of my good judgment. Again. "The roads are closed here. Send a helicopter to pick me up and I can be there in an hour."

A beat of silence followed. He'd won. So he capitulated. *Typical.* I pinched the bridge of my nose with two fingers.

Sounds of his even breathing traveled across the miles. "Since you're already there, you might consider doing your job."

My heart pounded and my nostrils flared. *Colonel Summer didn't show up. She didn't answer her phone, either. How'd you want me to interview her? Tarot cards?* I clamped my teeth together to keep my smart aleck retort to myself.

"This is not a secure line," he said. He'd not been able to deliver another secure cell phone to me since mine was destroyed in Charlotte, which was a blessing of sorts. I didn't trust him. He knew it. We both knew why. "Your lunch date should have details by now."

Major Clifton? Details about what? He didn't know anything about Jack Reacher that I hadn't already learned. I didn't need the Boss to micromanage my investigation.

"Anything else?" I stretched my neck and rolled my shoulders. The tension that had lodged there during the drive from Fort Bird was still with me.

"I sent you a file," he said, after a few more quiet moments. "Read it and contact me on a secure line for instructions."

Like finding a secure line to use in this place tonight would be possible. "Is that all?"

"Not quite," he said, with perhaps a bit of annoyance in his tone. "The next time I give you a direct order, follow it."

When he disconnected, I threw the phone onto the bed so hard it bounced off and landed on the floor and rolled under the mattress. I left it there.

CHAPTER NINE

I UNSCREWED THE TOP off the truck stop Cabernet, poured into one of the two Styrofoam cups, and connected my laptop to the secure satellite.

In my drop box was the new encrypted file, as promised.

The document was an official final court-martial disposition report to the then Army Chief of Staff from the Judge Advocate General's office. The fifty-page JAG report was dated June 1990.

Whole sections of the report were blacked out—redacted, which usually meant those contents were classified.

Flipping through quickly on the first pass I saw two names I recognized. Lieutenant Eunice Summer and Major Jack Reacher.

Reading what was not blacked out in the report didn't take long.

Lieutenant Summer had been the star witness in unspecified joint courts-martial of three Army officers, names and ranks redacted. Major Reacher had been her superior officer during the underlying investigation, but not mentioned otherwise. The report didn't specifically say what involvement Reacher had with the case, only that he was Summer's supervisor. Which could mean anything.

When the original case terminated with three officer arrests before the courts-martial, Reacher was immediately demoted to Captain and reassigned to Panama.

Summer assisted in the prosecutions. She continued in her role as Military Police Lieutenant through the "successful resolution of the matter," whatever that was.

Also included in the encrypted file was a short memo, unsigned. It stated that three months after the courts-martial was resolved, Lieutenant Summer was promoted to Captain. She was reassigned to Korea to serve directly under General Leon Garber. From earlier reports, I knew Garber was now deceased.

I unwrapped my dinner and refilled my wine cup and sat on the bed to think. The first bite of the sandwich had me regretting my rash refusal to have dinner with the Boss. There were many things about the nation's capital that I didn't care for, but no one could complain about the food. The second sandwich bite was worse than the first. I tossed it into the trash and rooted around in my bag for a protein bar.

The JAG report confirmed my hunch that the big professional changes Summer and Reacher experienced back then were connected. I munched the protein bar while I chewed the situation thoroughly until I knew three things for sure.

First, whatever happened at Fort Bird in early 1990 involved serious criminal activity. Nothing less would have resulted in the successful courts-martial of senior officers. Nor would Reacher have been busted or Summer promoted over a case involving enlisted personnel committing minor criminal infractions.

Second, the criminal activity, if it had become public back then, was clearly serious enough to have been a significant problem for the Army. Which meant that heads higher up the chain of command would have rolled. Maybe even have caused long-range damage to America's strategic interests abroad.

Third, because of these factors, the courts-martial were handled internally, confidentially, and swiftly. Prosecuting senior officers was never the Army's first choice. Such cases were devastating to morale. They also crushed the Army's reputation and, by spillover suspicion, the reputation of all high-level government agencies.

Which meant undisputable evidence of significant crimes must have existed against the officers beyond *all* doubt, not simply beyond a reasonable doubt.

Which could only mean that the officers confessed. After that, they were probably offered lighter sentences in exchange for silence. Otherwise, there would have been appeals and media attention. Neither of which had happened.

I refilled my wine glass and leaned back against the headboard.

How was Reacher involved in all of this? Again, after mulling things over, only three possibilities made any sense: Reacher was involved in committing the crimes, or he'd been the whistleblower, or he'd been a scapegoat. Maybe even all three, depending on the nature of the crimes.

Given the final disposition of Reacher's reduction in rank and Summer's promotion after the senior officers were sentenced, any combination of those three options were plausible.

Here was the kicker, though.

The Boss already knew about the 1990 crimes, the prosecutions, and Reacher's role in them before we were tasked to complete the Reacher file. Any one of the three options should have made Reacher unfit for whatever job the Boss had in mind.

The Boss had the necessary clearances for access to the full version of the JAG report. Which meant he was familiar with all of the facts of the case. He was older than Reacher and he might even have been aware of the courts-martial as those events occurred, back in 1990.

And yet, Reacher had not been immediately disqualified. And here I was. Partnered with Gaspar. Building the Reacher file. Tasked to discover his physical, mental, emotional, and financial fitness for a job with a security clearance so high that neither Gaspar nor I had access to the job's requirements. Looking for leads that could result in locating Reacher.

What kind of job could that be?

I'd finished the protein bar. A few more mouthfuls of the pathetic excuse for Cabernet and my body finally felt relaxed. My eyelids were heavy. The noise levels across the street at *The Lucky Bar* were still too loud, even though the heavy drapes were closed. Still, I might sleep a few hours and let my subconscious work on the problem.

A moment before I nodded off, I remembered the names of the JAG officers that were visible on the report.

One of them—the junior JAG—was new to me. Thomas O'Connor.

The senior JAG on the report had a name I had heard for the first time earlier today. Matthew Clifton.

Joe Reacher's West Point classmate.

Tony Clifton's brother.

CHAPTER TEN

Saturday 1:45 AM

WHICH CAME FIRST? THE screams or the gunshots? Two of
each jerked me awake from wine-induced oblivion. I was still
dressed and had not removed my shoes or my gun. I dashed to
the window, pushed the drapes aside and looked across the street
toward the noise.

Absolute bedlam had erupted around *The Lucky Bar*. Men
ran from inside and the knotted crowd outside was scattering like
a rack of billiard balls.

Two more gunshots blasted out from the bar.

I drew my weapon and picked up my phone and dialed 911
on my way out of the room. When the operator asked, "What is
your emergency?" I reported gunshots fired and two or more
ambulances required. The operator said she would dispatch
teams immediately.

Next, I called Major Clifton. His men were more than likely
patrons in *The Lucky Bar*. He'd want to know trouble had started
and local law enforcement would need the help. He didn't pick

up his cell and I left a message while I was still on the move.

I entered the stairwell next to the elevator and hopped down the stairs two at a time. At the bottom, the exterior emergency door would have dumped me outside too far from the bar. Instead, I powered through the wall-to-wall crowd in the lobby, which had grown by at least a hundred people in the hours since I'd elbowed my way through in the opposite direction.

Surely there was a limit to how many people could be stuffed into this room. Fire codes, at the very least, were certainly being violated. This group was now frighteningly chaotic, too. The din encouraged my pounding wine headache to ratchet up a few dozen decibels.

Scanning the jammed lobby as I plowed my way to the front entrance, I saw no guns drawn or injured victims inside this building. Which meant all of the shooting, screaming, and damage was happening across the road.

The second I stepped through the Grand Lodge exit into the frigid night, sleet peppered my skin relentlessly. I slid my feet along the icy sidewalk like a novice skater, unable to run or even hustle. Simply staying upright and balanced was challenge enough.

Patrons continued to flood from the exit at *The Lucky Bar*. It seemed like five hundred people had crowded into the place, and now all of them were climbing over each other to get out. Given the ice-sculpture garden the parking lot had become, most of the fleeing patrons were heading for the hotel, with a few members of the hotel crowd fighting the tide on their way to the club to help.

Predictably, the combination of alcohol consumption and icy pavement proved only slightly less treacherous for the panicked strip club refugees than the firefight had. All across the pitilessly rock-hard, ice-glazed sheet gleaming from the bar to the hotel across the highway, arms and legs pin-wheeled madly, bodies were upended, bones broke with sickeningly loud pops and snaps, all to the hellish accompaniment of wailing screams from figures writhing in agony on the ice.

I'd have stopped to help, but the continuing shooting inside was the top priority.

By the time I'd shuffle-weaved my way across the road through the carnage and approached the bar's entrance, I'd heard at least six more shots from inside. The music got louder the closer I slid. Ten yards away from the entrance, the wall of booze and stale cigarette smoke was still billowing out like an invisible, disgusting force field.

Until the locals arrived, it appeared that I was the only cop on the scene, and I had nothing remotely close to the muscle and firepower the situation required.

A wild-eyed man stood with his back glued to the wall just outside the open door, clearly too petrified to move. As I slid across the gaping doorway to him, the wall of booze-and-cigarette stench nearly knocked me over. Pounding music made quiet talk impossible, so I moved as close to him as I could get and leaned in to be heard.

"What's going on in there?" I shouted.

"Some crazy dude had a fight with one of the girls. He started shooting. The owner and the bouncer shot back." He shook his head rapidly from side to side. "It's chaos, man. People screaming, bleeding. Girls crying. I was in the back and I ran out, but then the ice—"

"The shooter. What's the shooter's name, do you know?"

He shook his head rapidly again. "Never saw him before in my life."

"Who's in charge here? The owner, the manager—you know his name?"

"Owner's Alvin. Him and kid, Junior, the bouncer, they been running *The Lucky* for years." He ran a hand hard over his head, and his feet started to slide out from beneath him on the ice. He slapped his palm onto the wall again as if it might glue him upright. He kept his feet. "They usually take care of things pretty good," he said, "but this dude's some kind of whack-job."

"And the woman? Is she his wife or girlfriend?"

"I don't know. Maybe. Lotta strangers around here tonight on account of the road bein' closed." He tilted his chin toward the Interstate instead of peeling one of his hands away from the wall to point.

I looked directly into his eyes. After a moment, he refocused on me. "I'm FBI Special Agent Kim Otto. What's your name?"

"Racine."

"Racine." I patted his arm. "I've called the police, but the storm will slow them down. You know this place. Can you help me out?"

"What, go back in there?" He shook his head violently from side to side, which moved his body away from the wall and caused his feet to slide again. When he'd twisted himself back into position, he said, "Are you crazy?"

Right. Crazy. Yes. For sure.

I took a deep breath. "Then can you at least stand here and keep everyone else outside? Don't let anyone come in until the police arrive. Can I count on you to do that?"

He didn't look happy about it, but he nodded. There was a fifty-fifty chance that he'd run as soon as my back was turned.

"Any military inside tonight?"

"Most nights some guys are here from Bird. Yeah, that's likely." Then he was shaking his head. "Maybe not, though. A night like this, they coulda been confined to base."

"If they're here, would they be armed?" Even as I heard the hope in my voice, the answer was obvious. If there were soldiers inside with weapons, this thing would already have been handled.

Racine shook his head. "Alvin don't allow no guns inside. He says booze and guns are a bad combination."

Alvin was a smart guy.

"Thanks." I patted his arm again and nodded. "Remember. Nobody comes in except the police."

I turned away from him and faced the doorway. The last gunshots had been fired a couple of minutes ago. Maybe the shooting was over. I flashed my head around the doorjamb for a quick look inside.

The only lights in the place were the pulsing red, blue, and green floodlights bathing the elevated stage near the center. Dancing poles, the stage. Not quite what I'd imagined when the truck stop deliverywoman brought my sandwich and wine three hours ago, but close enough.

Beyond that, the interior was too dark to see much except for the thick, stinking clouds of cigar and cigarette smoke layering the air. The music played at ear-splitting volume with a throbbing pulse, which my own blood began to rhythmically match.

Then I could make out a long bar across the front wall to my right, with liquor bottles, draft beer pulls and such in the usual places. The rest of the bar's floor space was filled with square tables and empty chairs. A dozen or more had been overturned, presumably when their occupants panicked and ran.

That's when I noticed the scrawny blonde dancer on her knees on the stage. Her naked skin was washed sickly green by the floodlight beaming down on her. Her forearms were flat on the stage and her head rested face down between them. Maybe she was praying. She definitely should have been. But from this distance, I couldn't tell.

Next, as my eyes continued to adjust to the scene, I saw splayed face down on the floor not far from the stage two men, each with double exit wounds, center mass, in the back. Their haircuts suggested they were Fort Bird residents.

And finally, behind the bar along the front wall to my right, were two men standing in the shadows. Both were about five-ten and well over two hundred pounds. The older guy was bald and wide all over. I couldn't see his face. The younger one was bulky. His tight black T-shirt fit like a second skin. His head was shaved. He had thick arms and tattooed forearms, but what I could see of his stomach was fairly trim, which made him seem oddly misshapen. Steroids, probably. Both held weapons aimed across the stage toward the back of the room.

I pulled my head back and flattened against the exterior wall next to my petrified sentry again to take stock of my meager assets and catalog limited options.

It had been maybe fifteen minutes since I'd heard the first shots and called 911. No help had arrived. I wore no body armor. Hell, I didn't even have a flashlight.

Going in there alone and without proper protection would be stupid.

But my hair hung in icicle strings. My suit stuck cold and clammy against my skin. My hands had begun to cramp around my gun.

I couldn't simply wait here until hypothermia set in hoping for divine intervention, either. Only one choice.

I took another deep breath, raised my gun. Falling on my ass wouldn't be helpful. I shuffled my shoes around the slick concrete, seeking and at last finding solid footing on the other side of the threshold.

One, two, three—before I reached *go*, more gunfire erupted inside. The first shots came from the back of the room, followed quickly by return fire from the front. The dancer screamed.

I scrambled back into position against the wall and out of the line of fire.

From this close, though still camouflaged by the incessant music, the shots were discernibly distinct. Three weapons, not four or more. Which meant the two men behind the bar outnumbered the one in the back shadows.

Retroactively counting the shots was impossible and served no useful purpose, as any of the three shooters could've reloaded. But all three must have had plenty of ammo at the start.

Just as I chanced another glance around the door frame, another round came from the back of the room. The older guy behind the bar grunted and fell back against the liquor bottles. He slapped his left palm against his right shoulder and fired back.

Junior let out some sort of crazy war cry and released rapid-fire rounds in the right direction.

The man in the back kept firing, too.

I ducked out again. My ears felt like they'd explode with the double percussion impact of noise and the music's rhythmic effect on my pounding heart.

Then, as abruptly as it had started, the shooting stopped again.

A beat passed. Two.

Now was my chance.

From the doorway, not because I expected it to make any difference, I yelled into the gale of deafening music, "FBI! FBI! Weapons down! We're coming in!"

CHAPTER ELEVEN

THE FIRST THING I noticed was the garish pink and green and blue floodlight wash that revealed the dancer, laid out on the floor of the stage. She was riddled with gunshot wounds. I counted six, but there could have been more. Her body had fallen onto her left side and dead eyes stared. Blood pooled under her stringy blonde hair.

I now realized it was the woman who had delivered my dinner from the truck stop a few hours ago. The medical examiner would sort out the bullets and determine which ones caused her death, but a shot to her head alone could have been fatal.

I kept my weapon ready as I squinted through the smoke layers. The two men on the ground with military haircuts that I'd seen from the doorway were not the only casualties. At least two more had fallen, from the looks of things while rushing the shooter.

He was dead, too. He'd blown back against the far wall, and now sat slumped over at the waist. The top of his head was missing.

Only Alvin and Junior, behind the bar, were still standing. I pointed my puny Sig Sauer directly at them, wishing I had a missile launcher, and, taking advantage of a comparative lull in their insane sound system's assault, shouted as loud as I could, "FBI! Guns down! Hands in the air!"

"Or what?" Junior bellowed, waving his weapon my way, muzzle up. "You're no bigger than a minute. What do you think you can do to me?"

Good question. My bullets might slow him down or even stop him. But he'd have plenty of time to kill me first.

Alvin raised his injured right arm and swung his open hand and slapped Junior on the ear hard enough to knock him sideways. "Watch your mouth and do what she told you."

Junior regained his balance. As the music surged with renewed fury around us, he placed his weapon on the bar and raised his hands. Alvin put his down and raised one arm slightly. The other arm didn't seem functional. Maybe the slap to Junior's head had triggered additional damage to it. Blood ran down onto his hand and dripped onto the floor.

"Turn that music off!" I yelled.

Junior reached to the side of the bar and pressed something. The instant silence was a shock to my system. My blood had been pounding with the music's rhythm and the sudden stop hit me like a quick side-fist punch to the heart.

"Come out from behind the bar. Slowly." My voice sounded muffled and weak and raspy, probably from all the yelling. Or maybe my voice was normal and the problem was damage to my eardrums. "Keep your hands high."

They walked as instructed. Alvin limped badly on his right leg, but I couldn't see a bleeding wound anywhere. I didn't have handcuffs with me, but even if I had, they'd never have encircled Junior's massive wrists.

"Sit down here." I pointed to two chairs close enough to the exit that I could hastily retreat, should the need arise.

They sat. As long as they wanted to do what I asked, we'd be fine.

How the hell long can it possibly take to get some squad cars out here, anyway?

"Don't worry," Alvin said. His shoulder was oozing blood, but he acted as if he couldn't feel it. "Ain't nobody left inside here to cause more trouble tonight. Everbody's run out or dead. You call the sheriff and the medics?"

"They're on their way." I didn't lower my gun or move my gaze even a fraction.

"Good." Alvin lowered his chin to his chest like he'd run out of steam.

The last thing I needed was to lose him now. But if I moved any closer to deliver any kind of emergency aid, I'd be within easy striking distance. If Alvin clubbed me the way he'd clubbed Junior on the side of the head, he'd knock me into next week.

The best I could do was try to keep him talking.

"Tell me what happened here tonight."

Alvin lifted his head and shifted in his seat to look at me. The move pulled his head out of the shadows into a blue wash pulsing spotlight and I got my first clear look at him. I clamped my mouth shut to hold back the gasp.

His face was covered with old straight razor scars. The cuts had been deep. The white scars crisscrossed over most of his forehead, both cheeks, and his chin. The scars glowed in the spotlight. His nose had been broken several times. It looked like a blob in the center of the latticed scars. His brows were gnarled and the eyes beneath them were the smallest things on his face.

No way would I want to meet either of these two anywhere without a full clip in my gun.

Again, I said, "Tell me what happened here tonight."

"Guy wanted one of the girls. She didn't want him." Alvin shrugged. "He wouldn't take no for an answer."

"Did you know him?"

"He was probably just passing through. Got stuck here like everybody else. Drank too much." He shrugged again. "It happens."

I believed him. *The Lucky Bar* was the kind of place where fights were common. He should have had medics on retainer.

Alvin looked toward the bodies. "Some of these boys was soldiers. You call out to Bird, too? Get the MPs on the way?"

"I did."

"Good." Alvin lowered his chin again as if he knew how extremely unpleasant his face was to watch.

"What about the woman?" My questions were partly to keep him occupied and partly to be sure he remained conscious. His blood loss was a problem. If the medics didn't arrive soon, he could lose the arm, for sure. Or lose more than that.

"Gloria. She hadn't been workin' here very long. She was always a quiet one since she was a girl."

"Gloria was a local woman?"

"Until she married."

"I noticed your limp. Were you shot in the leg, too?"

Alvin looked up at me again. He blinked his tiny eyelids. His eyes looked like raisins in a giant dough ball. "Naw. Old injury to my knee. Twenty years back. I got the knee replaced, but the bones and muscles don't work right."

Junior glared at me like an angry Rottweiler. "And one of

these days, we'll find the asshole who did that, too." His voice was curiously high-pitched for a big man. Steroids were probably responsible for that, too.

"What do you mean?"

"He was passin' through. Ain't never been back." He stuck out his chin. His smallish hands flexed into fists on top of his massive thighs. "But the Army ain't protectin' him no more. Big, bad, cheap-shotting MP." He sneered. "Won't be neither so big or nor so bad once we find him. The bigger they are, the harder they fall."

Big, bad, MP? Twenty years ago? "Do you know his name?" The frissons running up and down my central nervous system foretold the answer.

"Reacher. Jack Reacher." He must've seen interest in my eyes because his eyes lit in return. "Oh, you *know* him. You know him?"

I shook my head. "Never met the man."

But he wasn't buying. "You see him," he said, "you tell him to watch his back."

On the list of Army don'ts that got Reacher busted back, Major Clifton had included civilian complaints. Reacher was only at Fort Bird a short time and he'd managed to make more enemies than a terrorist. No surprise.

Sirens wailed in the distance, moving toward *The Lucky Bar*, but they weren't closing the gap fast enough. I stepped to the doorway and looked outside. Several people were still down on the pavement, but others were trying to render aid.

I counted seven men and two women injured on the ground. Others seemed to be simply waiting on the ground because standing on the ice was impossible.

I turned back and tilted my head toward the bodies inside the bar. "Will you sit here while I check on the others, Alvin? Can I trust you and Junior to do that?"

Alvin nodded. "We ain't goin' nowhere. Got nowhere to go."

"Ain't got much left here, neither," Junior added.

"You have any overhead lights?"

Alvin pointed with his chin to a side wall near the bar. I walked a few steps and flipped the lights on.

The Lucky Bar had looked a lot better in the dark.

The place had been old and damaged before tonight's melee destroyed everything beyond repair. The tables and chairs had been mismatched when they found their way to the bar at least three decades ago. They were chipped, broken, covered with the scars of a tough business. The stage was a shoddy affair, too.

I walked across the concrete floor, sticky with spilled booze, congealing blood, and other bodily fluids I didn't want to dwell upon. To be sure, I checked for a pulse on all six bodies, the four soldiers, the dancer, and the gunman. As expected. Nothing.

From the back of the room, where I stood near the gunman's body still slumped against the wall, I looked up to see Major Anthony Clifton walk through the door. A local cop was with him.

Clifton moved right past Alvin and Junior without stopping, heading toward the soldiers. He knelt to check carotid pulses with the same results I'd confirmed.

The local cop approached me. He was about sixty and fit, like a runner who lifted weights, too. A little under six-feet, maybe one-sixty or so. He wore the uniform well. Even the wide-brimmed hat suited him.

"Sheriff," I nodded and held out my badge. A quick look was all he required. Most law enforcement officers know an FBI badge when they see one. "Special Agent Kim Otto."

"Randy Taylor." He looked down at the dead gunman. "What happened here?"

"Alvin says this guy wanted that woman and when she refused, he started shooting." My adrenaline levels had been falling to normal since the shooting stopped and I realized all of a sudden how freaking wet and cold I was, even in the hot room. My whole body was shaking. I had to clamp my teeth to still the chattering.

Taylor kept scanning, completing his own professional appraisal, presumably. "That seem like the truth to you?"

"I was asleep in my room across the road when the shots woke me up. I called 911 and Major Clifton. By the time I got here, everything was almost over."

"You fire your weapon?" Taylor asked. "If you did, we'll need to take it."

"No chance to." I shook my head and handed over my weapon so he could confirm and didn't argue. We both knew the rules. "The shooting was over by the time I came inside."

"We'll want to talk to you for more details." He seemed to see me for the first time. My wet clothes, chattering teeth, and blue skin. He checked my weapon and gave it back.

Clifton walked up. "We'll have plenty to do tonight, Randy. She'll freeze to death if she doesn't get a hot shower and warmer clothes. You're at the Grand Lodge across the street, aren't you?"

I nodded.

"Check in with me before you leave town, Agent Otto?" It was a request. He had no authority over me.

I nodded again through my chattering teeth and turned to leave. Clifton bowed his head closer to me. "I'll report to the locals and call you in an hour."

Processing the crime scene would take a while, and processing the carnage would take weeks. There would be plenty of time for me to answer questions and ask a few of my own. Starting with what had happened between Jack Reacher and Alvin way back when. But the feud was old. My questions could wait. Assuming I didn't freeze to death first.

"Works for me." I holstered my gun and made my way out of the bar, navigated its frozen parking lot, the glazed highway, and the hotel's parking lot, sleet lacing me every step of the way. By the time I trudged through the lobby and up the stairs and stepped into a steaming hot shower, my entire body was colder than a frozen turkey.

CHAPTER TWELVE

NINETY MINUTES LATER, WHEN Major Clifton arrived
with two huge Styrofoam cups of hot black coffee from the truck
stop, I could have kissed him with gratitude. It was late and we
were both exhausted but keyed up, too. The hot shower had
reheated my body, but he was still wet and cold. I sat on the bed
and he paced the room trying to warm up.

"What's going on out there now?"

I knew most of the answer. While I'd waited for him, I'd
opened the heavy drapes and watched some of the show. I'd seen
the arrival and departure of several medical trucks, Highway
Patrol and local police vehicles from New Haven and the county.
Uniformed officers were now posted at the entrance to *The
Lucky Bar*. Crime scene processing had already begun and the
familiar yellow tape was slashed across the doorway.

Through everything, water in various stages of freezing
continued to fall. Temperatures must have fallen slightly since I
left the scene because the ground was now dusted with white.
Snow over ice is among the most treacherous possible driving
conditions. Processing tonight's crime scene and handling the

victims would be more complicated and difficult until the weather cleared.

Clifton ran a flat palm across his face, which was showing a day's growth of beard. He replied in the formal way he might report to a superior officer. "All of the injured civilians have been transported to the hospital. I have MPs on the scene to assist Sheriff Taylor. We located no additional injured Army personnel. The homicides will be processed by civilian law enforcement. Sherriff Taylor is a good cop. He'll do what needs to be done."

He stopped pacing a moment and turned to face me. "The case isn't my jurisdiction, so I have no choice in any event."

I nodded. "What about the bartender and the bouncer? I assume they were arrested for opening fire on the shooter, just to keep track of them until things get sorted out if nothing else."

"Taylor sent Junior to the local jail. But Alvin required medical attention, probably surgery to that shoulder, so he was arrested and then transported to the hospital." He turned his head again to watch events across the road.

"Did you interview them before Taylor got ahold of them?"

"A little bit. I've been the XO at Bird for about a year, so I've had dealings with both of them before. Alvin is a decent guy who's had a tough life. *The Lucky Bar* is all he has to support himself and his family. He'll reopen as soon as possible."

In my experience, places like *The Lucky Bar* operated on a thin line barely inside the law. On any given night, there were plenty of chances for trouble of one kind or another. Judging from the response to that gunman tonight, Alvin and Junior expected trouble and were prepared to handle it.

"Seems like Alvin was pretty lucky to me."

"How so?"

"Neither he nor his son are dead. The gunshot wound to his shoulder will give him some problems, but it appeared treatable. Lots of folks, including at least four soldiers from your base who were trying to do the right thing, weren't that lucky tonight."

Clifton squared his shoulders and leaned his back against the window. "I could have made the place off-limits to enlisted men. I've threatened to do it more than once. I could've confined them to the base tonight because of the weather, and I thought about it."

"But you didn't do any of that."

"You drove here from Bird. How many five-star restaurants and symphony halls did you see along the way?" He paused and raised his cup again. "The Army's not an easy gig. We train hard. We expect fewer soldiers to do a lot more. The discipline is tough. People need an outlet and we can't provide everything on the base, as much as I wish we could."

I understood his point. Compromises had to be made. Enlisted personnel were entitled to free time. They were going to spend it somewhere.

The Lucky Bar was reasonably close and somewhat manageable for the MPs. Maybe everything in the place wasn't strictly legal, but there were worse places they could go.

And, until tonight, when four of Bird's personnel were killed, worse things could have happened when soldiers went farther afield.

I asked, "Do you know anything about the shooter yet? Or the dancer?"

"Shooter had a Tennessee driver's license in his wallet and a few credit cards. A little bit of cash on him, not much. His name was Jeffrey Mayne. Mean anything to you?"

"No."

"Alvin doesn't keep the best records on his employees, so we're not sure about her yet. She grew up here in New Haven, but she'd been gone for ten years. She told Alvin her name was Gloria Bedazzle, which he simply accepted because he didn't remember her at first. Said she was looking to escape an abuser. It was probably instinct that brought her back where Alvin could at least try to look out for her. Alvin has always been a sucker for those stories."

He again rubbed a palm over his face. "Alvin should know better. He's been in the business long enough. He knew the ex would come looking for her and the outcome would be ugly."

Meaning that Alvin's response to the gunman was premeditated, at least. Racine said Alvin didn't allow guns in *The Lucky Bar*, but he'd let Jeffrey Mayne bring one inside. And both Alvin and Junior were only too willing to shoot back.

"So you think this was a personal problem between the star-crossed lovers that got out of hand. Straight homicidal mania?"

"Seems like it now. When our guys rushed Mayne, they might have made the situation worse." Dark circles marked his eyes and deeper lines ran toward his mouth. Gone was the sexy dude I'd first met back at Bird. This guy was grim and exhausted. "It's hard to say until we have more facts from the witnesses. And from the medical examiner."

My gut said Tony was probably right. The final report would contain final conclusions, but right now there was no evidence to suggest anything other than a domestic argument gone wrong. Any cop on any beat in any jurisdiction will tell you that there's nothing more dangerous than responding to a domestic disturbance.

And if this was ruled a domestic disturbance, the case would be handled appropriately and had absolutely nothing to do with me or my assignment. Which meant that none of it—Alvin and Junior and the shoot-out at *The Lucky Bar*—was my concern.

So I moved on to something that was my business. "Junior told me that Alvin's bad knee was the result of a fight with Jack Reacher. You know anything about that?"

Clifton's left eyebrow lifted, but he didn't respond.

"What about Colonel Summer?" I pressed. "She was there. She's got to know all about it, doesn't she?"

"That's why I wanted to talk to you privately. To deliver the rest of the bad news." He paused a moment, maybe looking for a way to soften harsh words. Finding none, he simply reported the facts. "Fifty minutes before you arrived at Fort Bird this morning, Colonel Summer's car was crushed between two semi-trucks. A chain reaction collision. On the highway. Mile marker #224, between here and the Fort Bird exit. Experience says Colonel Summer was dead in less than half a second."

"Experience?" I held my expression steady, but the news jolted my stomach. Of all the things I'd expected him to say, "Summer's dead" was nowhere on my list. Dead in a vehicle crash less than an hour before she was supposed to spill everything she knew to the FBI? Way too convenient.

Whatever Summer had learned about Reacher back then, whatever she knew about his life after he left the Army, might have died with her. More than a million active and inactive co-workers became instant suspects in her death, but my money was betting on her connection to one particular big, bad MP being at the center.

CHAPTER THIRTEEN

TONY SHARED THE REMAINING facts. How Summer had been on the way to meet me from her office in Rock Creek, Virginia. Driving like a bat out of hell, as was her well-known habit. How she'd rear-ended the tanker going 80 per and then the long-haul driver behind her had nowhere else to go except over the side to the deep valley floor below. The driver said he considered going off the road, but concluded his suicide wouldn't help the small woman in the already crushed sports car. He'd have been right.

The details of the crash weren't really that important. About ninety people die in car crashes every day in the United States, give or take, according to the National Highway Traffic Safety Administration. Not as common as fatal heart attacks, but common enough that news outlets don't report vehicular fatalities unless somebody famous was drunk, high, or dead.

Summer wasn't a celebrity of any kind. Tony had brought her personnel file with him, along with the rest of the already fattening file on the crash that had killed her. She'd left no children or parents or ex-spouses. She had a passel of siblings and cousins scattered about, as relatives usually are. She was a serious, dedicated Military Police Officer, one of the best the U.S. Army had produced in the past twenty-five years, based on that file. Her death wouldn't rate a two-sentence mention anywhere except in the military press and her church bulletin.

Not that honoring or mourning her would make a difference to my assignment. Colonel Eunice Summer was dead. Not even the Boss could bring her back to life.

Several things clicked into place in my head. Like why the Boss didn't give me the JAG report before my scheduled interview with Summer. He'd certainly possessed it before she died. He could have provided the redacted version to me earlier if he'd wanted to so I could've been farther along on my Reacher file by now.

He wouldn't have sent me to Colonel Summer in the first place unless he knew she could fill in a few blanks. But when she no-showed, he hunted her down and found out why. When he learned that she'd died and could never reveal what she knew about Reacher, he intended me to go after the Intel another way. He meant me to use the JAG file instead of whatever he'd expected Summer to tell me. Like Summer was another chess piece removed from his board and nothing more.

That didn't sit right with me. Not at all.

"You're sure that's how it happened? She was driving too fast on the slick pavement and rear-ended a tanker? Going eighty miles an hour? And you're sure it's her?"

"That's why you couldn't reach me when you called tonight. I was at the crash site. I saw the car." He paused. "I saw the body. You can pull up news footage on the Internet. It's been on all the stations tonight."

"You feel confident that's all there was to her death, then?"

He raised both eyebrows this time instead of one. "What else would it be?"

"Dunno." I shook my head. "Maybe she was impaired. Was she a drinker? Drugs?"

"If she was impaired, the autopsy would discover that, but she wasn't, and it won't. So what's next?" His eyes widened. "Are you imagining that Summer would have committed suicide by slamming into that tanker just to avoid telling you ancient history about Jack Reacher? That's a bit absurd, don't you think?"

Actually, no. The Reacher investigation had proved to be bizarre and unpredictable. I'd already seen crazier things than a staged accident happen where Reacher was involved. I shrugged. "I'm going to need to see those reports."

"The FBI has access to anything and everything these days. More access than I have." His voice was stiff, offended, which I found curious. "But you'll have to wait. The coroner's going to be a little busy for the next few days."

Now he sounded full-on pissed.

"Look," I said. "I'm not trying to sully the stellar reputation of an Army hero here."

"That's how I heard it." He'd stuffed his hands into his pockets and his entire body seemed to close up tight.

Yep. Totally miffed. Read that one right.

"I was really looking forward to meeting Colonel Summer and I'm so sorry for your loss." I drained the last of my coffee and placed the empty cup on the floor, which was the only flat surface available besides my bed and the bathroom vanity. "But put your professional hat on here and not your personal one."

"Meaning?" He sounded petulant like a child saying *Oh, yeah? Well, make me!*

"Three unusual things happened here within the past fifteen

hours. Two were extraordinary things. Terrible things. The third—which was really the first of them—might have been just an interesting coincidence." I kept my voice level, reasonable. "You're a cop. Don't tell me you believe in coincidence."

He shook his head and his quills seemed to settle into place a little. "I am not following you. Sorry."

"Unusual event number one: that bloodbath across the street. *The Lucky Bar* has been operating for decades in exactly the same location and exactly the same way." I'd lay it out, one element at a time, watching his prickly reactions to be sure he followed the logic. "You told me that Alvin has always been a sucker for domestic abuse victims. Which means that angry exes of all types, some with homicidal intent, have no doubt come stalking in the past. Alvin has handled them. He's never had a mass shooting in the bar before. True?"

"Yes." Clipped. Unfriendly. But not quite as hostile.

I moved on. "Number two: Colonel Summer's death on that mountain road. Think about it. Colonel Summer was posted at Fort Bird for five years, and she told me she was now investigating a corruption case at Bird, too. So she had driven that highway dozens if not hundreds of times, in all types of weather. According to her personnel file, Colonel Summer was known to be an excellent driver though her speeding habit was as well documented as her expertise. Everyone who knew her was aware of both her driving skill and her penchant for speed."

He shrugged his assent, but his steady gaze never wavered. No epiphany related to the identity of the third item lightened his scowl.

You can lead a cop to water, but you can't make him think. I applied patience and waited for him to make the connections himself.

He was a smart guy. He'd been in the business long enough. He had seen every kind of crime there was and all of his suspects were trained killers. Nobody built a resume like that by accepting coincidence as any kind of answer to anything.

He sighed. "You think the bar shooting and the crash happened today because FBI Special Agent Kim Otto came to Fort Bird to interview Colonel Eunice Summer." The defensive tension lines in his face slowly faded and his shoulders relaxed. If he hadn't been so totally undone by the events of his day, he might even have smiled. "You're good at your job, Otto. I checked before we allowed you on base. But your conclusions seem a bit grandiose to me."

When he put it that way, he missed the point by a mile. I shook my head. "Not exactly."

"What, then? Exactly."

My orders were to stay off the books and under the radar. I wouldn't tell him anything more. He'd figure it out, or he wouldn't. Either way, he was on his own.

"Anything else going on across the road over there?" I asked.

When he turned his head toward the window to check, I pushed off the bed, stood and stretched and pulled an antacid out of my pocket and popped it into my mouth. Nothing worse than coffee on an empty stomach after a bottle of cheap red wine and twelve gallons of adrenaline to get my stomach snake thrashing.

I felt my phone vibrate in my pocket for the third time since Clifton had arrived.

"Looks like they've removed all the civilians from the parking lot and secured the area," he reported. "Crime scene will be there for a while." He dropped his cup into my trashcan and walked to the door. "I have to get back."

"Thanks for the coffee," I said as he turned the doorknob and stepped into the corridor. "I'm very sorry about Colonel Summer, Tony. I was really looking forward to meeting her."

He'd turned, but his demeanor felt almost as frosty as the snow falling outside. He nodded again, then walked toward the elevator without a backward glance. The door snugged closed behind him.

He would figure out that Reacher's old case was at the center of everything. He was that kind of guy. The kind who would investigate whether he believed my theories or not.

And when he caught up with the facts and the logic, he would call. He might even have something useful to add. Until then, Gaspar and I were on our own.

I pulled my phone out of my pocket. I'd received three text messages while Clifton was here. One from Gaspar and two from the Boss.

Gaspar's had come first. "American #7392. Nashville. 1115. I'll get a car." That last bit made me grin. Of course, Gaspar would get a car. Which translated into a big old boat of a vehicle. He'd walk before he'd be caught dead driving a little SUV like the one I'd rented in Charlotte. He was number two and number two always drove and the driver needed to be comfortable, he said.

Next were two texts from the Boss. The first said: "Confirmed. Delta #846. Departs Charlotte 0945. Secure files available."

I replied, "OK."

The Boss's second text confirmed my earlier suspicion that he couldn't actually see inside this hotel room, and he couldn't hear my conversations here, either. He texted: "Summer. Deceased."

He'd known about Colonel Summer's death hours ago and he hadn't told me. When I called Major Clifton about the shooting at *The Lucky Bar*, the Boss knew I'd find out about Summer. So he'd sent the second text *after* Major Clifton had delivered the news instead of before.

Which confirmed, again, that Gaspar was right. The Boss wasn't God and he didn't know everything.

It also confirmed that he was only reliable when he felt like it.

My reply to the Boss's text was, as the Brits say, cheeky. "Suspicious circumstances. Please collect reports."

I checked my Seiko for the time. It was already five o'clock. The drive from here to the Charlotte airport was 126 miles. It would take more than two hours in this weather, according to the GPS.

Which meant Gaspar's flight would be on the ground in Nashville for at least half an hour before I could get there.

I quickly connected to the secure satellite and downloaded the new files to read on the plane. I watched the news footage of Summer's crash and downloaded that, too. Then I collected the few items I'd brought with me, stuffed them into my bags, and tossed my room key onto the bed on my way out.

I was already on the road when I remembered two things I should not have missed. First, Tony Clifton didn't answer my question. I'd asked, "You feel confident her death was an accident, then?" He'd replied, "What else would it be?" Not a lie, exactly. But a diversion. He knew something more and I should have followed up. The Boss would know. I made a mental note to ask him if I couldn't find the answer another way.

Second, I still hadn't opened that flat manila envelope from the sentry at the Fort Bird exit gate. I'd do that on the plane, too.

CHAPTER FOURTEEN

THE FORMER LESLEY BROWNING, and perhaps former Mrs. Joe Reacher, now lived in a suburb thirty minutes due west of Nashville, Tennessee. The non-stop flight from Charlotte was less than two hours in the air on a Canadair CRJ 700. Only sixty-six passengers aboard. The three-man crew consisted of a pilot, a co-pilot, and one flight attendant.

In my line of work, flying was as necessary as a root canal and nowhere near as pleasant. People who are not afraid to fly tell me fear of flying is irrational. They say flying is safer than driving a car or riding a bike. They are idiots.

Planes make powerful weapons; we all know that too well. They're also machines that can fail like every other machine. They are operated by humans, none of whom is perfect. And planes are no match for Mother Nature.

But the worst thing about planes is that I wasn't in control of the flight, which meant evasive maneuvers were never an option.

I tightened my lap belt, placed an antacid on my tongue and pressed it to the roof of my mouth, closed my eyes, and clenched the armrests for takeoff.

Once we were airborne and were at an altitude as safe as we were going to get for portable electronic devices, I unencrypted and opened the Boss's file. The summary report for Joe [none] Reacher was first. Not much new. Most of it was information we'd uncovered when our assignment began.

Why had Stan and Josephine Reacher been opposed to middle names, I wondered again? Neither brother owned one.

I skimmed the data. Basic statistical information included date of birth and death. Joe had died in the field in the line of duty at thirty-eight. Not long after his brother left the Army and turned up in Margrave, Georgia.

Joe Reacher had enrolled in and graduated from West Point two years before his brother.

After West Point, Joe served in Army Intelligence. In my experience, no one serving in that position was likely to have been a saint. Those guys were laser-focused on the necessary and unencumbered by niceties. Joe's file from those days was probably scrubbed as clean as his brother's. I'd asked for it several times. The Boss said Joe Reacher's Army Intelligence file was classified, which it likely was.

After that, Joe had moved into another classified and undisclosed position at Treasury, where he was working on January 10, 1990, when his mother Josephine died in Paris at the age of sixty. The only thing new to me here was that both Jack and Joe Reacher attended Josephine's funeral on January 14, four days after her death.

A quick memory check confirmed that Jack Reacher had left Fort Bird for the last time on the day before he buried his mother. I made a note to check his flights. He could have arrived in Paris early, but he might have been doing something else between Fort Bird and Paris, too.

There was nothing in Joe Reacher's file about Lesley Browning. No indication their marriage had ever happened or been terminated, which made me feel better. At least I hadn't missed a lead as obvious as an ex-wife for no reason. Records should exist somewhere, but finding them would take time and effort, which I hoped would not be necessary. My plan was to go right to the source.

As requested, the Boss had located Lesley Browning, formerly of Newburgh, New York, the childhood home of Matthew and Anthony Clifton, not far from West Point. The encrypted file contained basic information about Lesley. She was a year younger than Joe, which meant they were both old enough to marry without parental consent at the time the union was purported to have been made.

Whether they had ever married or not, she should have known things about Joe that no one else had told us. Which could lead me to something relevant about Jack. Which could lead, well, anywhere.

Or nowhere. Again.

Looking at the pathetically slim connection with a clear eye from 40,000 feet, chasing down Lesley Browning seemed like a stupid idea. She was just a kid back then. Barely eighteen. Her marriage to Joe, if it had taken place, had been brief. She was married again now, with children. What could she possibly know that would help complete the Reacher file all these years later?

But we were on the way and there was no going back and nowhere else to go if we did turn back. Only one choice. Again.

I'd traveled the still icy and treacherous highway where Colonel Summers died on the way to the Charlotte airport, white knuckled and nervous the whole time. As I watched the downloaded news footage again on my laptop, I imagined what the crash must have been like for her.

Speed kills. Maybe those were Eunice Summer's last thoughts if she had time to think at all. She was running late and traveling eighty miles an hour in a fifty-mile-an-hour zone when she slammed into the tanker. She was an excellent driver, but also a notorious lead foot who'd been warned a million times. Maybe that thought flashed into her head, too, half-an-instant before impact.

Then again, if the tanker hadn't been there, she'd have been fine.

And even if it *was* there—and it definitely was—why in the hell did a driver as skilled as Summer simply plow into it?

Several factors contributed to the perfect setup for catastrophe. That section of Interstate banked on a steep, widening curve. Rain slicked the asphalt. Light fog settled over the road. Even if I'd been familiar with the road, I would have slowed to the fifty-mile-an-hour speed limit, at least, but I was no expert driver like Summer. Maybe she'd considered it a challenge or something.

No skid marks extended even a short, wavy distance behind her car. Even with both feet standing on the brake applying every ounce of strength she owned, she'd been running way too fast to lay a long trail of rubber in between rounding that bend and flattening her vehicle and herself into the truck.

But still. Not even a Sharpie-stroke's worth of a skid mark?

The marks left by the tires of the double tractor-trailer rushing down the mountain incline behind her jaunty red sports car were a damn sight longer. Proving the driver tried to stop, but failed. Not that it mattered. She never felt the second hit.

The captain jarred me from reliving Summer's crash when he turned on the seatbelt sign and chimes from overhead indicated our initial descent into Nashville. We'd hit some bumpy air on the way down, he said. Lovely. I closed the files and my laptop and prepared for landing.

I'd been stuck in seat 1A, the worst seat on any plane. 1A was Gaspar's seat. I hated 1A. Too much open space around 1A. From 1A, I could see the galley and the door to the flight deck. I could hear the flight attendants talking among themselves or on the phone with the cockpit crew. In 1A I'd be the first to know when something went wrong.

Usually, of course, absolutely nothing went wrong. And the good news about 1A was that I could hear when the landing gear was up and locked or down and locked—among the best sounds on any flight, second only to hearing my feet firmly strike the ground.

As the Canadair CRJ 700 struggled with the promised turbulence, I ran through my standard rationalizations. Flying was safer than driving. Only a small percentage of flights actually crashed and eighty-two percent of plane crashes were non-fatal. I'd already survived three crashes, which meant I was a lucky flyer, for sure.

Then again, forty-seven percent of fatal accidents occurred during final approach and landing. But I ignored that statistic whenever possible.

The flight attendants rushed down the aisle checking seatbelts and tray tables and seat backs, hanging on to avoid falling. The beverage trays the attendant on my side of the plane had left on the galley counter bounced onto the floor and coffee, juices, and water splashed everywhere.

When the attendant reached the crew's jump seat and

buckled in, her face looked a little green, though probably not as green as mine.

My hands clenched the armrests instinctively on the first bump. I braced my feet flat on the floor. I kept my eyes open and nausea at bay through sheer force.

The plane then bounced hard enough to jam my teeth together. A baby seated somewhere behind me squalled. The first baby's cries encouraged another child to scream.

More equally hard bounces followed the first and more passengers joined the children in their screaming each time.

And then, we were swooping up into the air again, leaving my stomach somewhere down near the tarmac.

The captain's smooth voice came on again. "Folks, we're having some difficulty with the landing gear in the nose of the aircraft. We're going to circle the runway and give the gear one more opportunity to deploy correctly. We may have a bumpy landing, but we'll have you on the ground safely in just a few minutes. Please stay in your seats with your seat belts securely fastened."

Difficulty with the landing gear? Difficulty could mean anything from a flat tire to no landing gear at all. Any difficulty with landing gear could be disastrous, but the landing gear in the *nose*? Worse still.

I closed my eyes and tried not to think about the last time I'd been on a plane with malfunctioning landing gear and we'd ended up with an emergency evacuation on an air slide.

The plane's slow circle and final approach was punctuated by the sounds of landing gear grinding but not locking into place after several tries. The motors whined repeatedly and too long.

From 1A, I couldn't see the ground outside even if I'd had the nerve to try. But I'd been to Nashville many times. It is a mountain city, not a coastal town. Belly-landings on the hard ground were a lot less survivable than skimming the Hudson River's surface.

Finally, the landing gear's grinding whine changed. The captain spoke to us again. "Folks, we've got the nose gear down and locked. It'll be bumpy, but we'll be fine. Remain seated and braced for landing."

A cheer from the other passengers, but not from me. I'd noticed he didn't say the nose gear was operating perfectly.

The pilot touched down and braked and the plane began to slow and the nose gear did not snap off and drop us to our fiery ends. After the longest seconds of my life, the Canadair CRJ 700 came to a complete stop, all in one piece. Once again passengers exploded with laughter and applause and, this time, happy tears from the adults. Even I joined in the celebration, taking my first full breath since our initial failure to rejoin the planet's surface.

Summer's imagined last moments rose up in me once again, even as I'd survived yet another battle with the gods of air travel with nothing worse than bruises. There was no ice on the runway and no deer on the road and no enormous vehicle ten times heavier than the CRJ 700 sitting in front of us. Unlike Summer, my survival had been in the hands of experts. I'd been lucky.

Even so, we weren't safe yet. Something was seriously wrong because the flight attendant hustled us off the plane down the emergency chute where ground crews whisked us away from the disabled bird on wobbly legs. I'd had no chance to shake the pilot's hand and slobber with gratitude. Nor did I hang around for the debriefing, apologies, and offers for flight coupons.

By the time I made my way outside the Nashville International Airport terminal into yet another cold November afternoon, I'd seen several televisions broadcasting video of our breathtaking landing. I didn't stop to hear the blow-by-blow. I'd already lived it and that was more than enough.

Gaspar was waiting at the curb behind the wheel of an old Crown Vic. Who knows where he'd acquired it. The full-sized brown tank was always his first choice and my last. I bent to knock on the passenger window and jerked my left thumb toward the back.

He popped the trunk. I stowed my bag and joined him inside the cabin. The whole process was as fluid as an Olympic gymnast's performance and took half the time.

"Good to see you survived the flight, Suzie Wong." He grinned and waited while I settled into the front passenger seat. Gaspar didn't have a mean bone in his body. He didn't know how close we'd come to not meeting right here and right now. If he'd known, he wouldn't have joked like that, and I was glad not to talk about it yet.

"Right back atcha, Chico." I pulled an alligator clamp out of my pocket and secured it to the shoulder harness at the retractor to avoid beheading on sudden stops. I left the wings of the clamp open to be sure it would fly off and the belt would grab in the event of an actual catastrophe.

I avoided thinking about how no seat belt would have helped us if our pilot had been less skilled or lucky, and how no safety restraint in her red sports car would have saved Eunice Summer, either.

When it's your time, it's your time. Summer the speed demon had tempted fate once too often and she finally lost. I made a mental note to remember that.

CHAPTER FIFTEEN

WHEN I LEANED AGAINST the seatback, I could barely see over the Crown Vic's long hood. Once again, I felt like a child in need of a booster seat. My breathing continued to even out as my heart rate slowed to near normal. It was good to have him behind the wheel now instead of me.

Gaspar smirked and watched my process, and after I'd straightened myself out, he gestured to my cup holder. "The coffee's a present from me"—he tossed a small padded envelope into my lap—"and that's one from the Boss."

He shifted the slow boat into drive and lumbered away from the curb.

Experience, along with heft and weight, told me what was inside the envelope. A secure cell phone complete with the latest and greatest FBI monitoring equipment installed. I tossed the envelope into the back seat, where it landed next to Gaspar's identical unopened one.

My mind flashed to another envelope, this one the same color, but larger and flat. The one I'd received from the sentry at Fort Bird on the way out yesterday, still unopened, too. I shrugged. That envelope was stowed in my bag in the trunk where I couldn't get to it until we stopped again.

I took a grateful sip of the hot java. "So how's Maria? And little man Gaspar?"

"Maria's tired. She's got our daughters and her family with her, for now." He'd frowned and then his mouth lifted up at the corner. "Little man Gaspar is still being stubborn. Looks like it'll be a while before he joins us. Docs are saying it could be two weeks past her due date."

I sighed. "Men. Never ready when we are."

"Hey, keep it clean in here. This vehicle is G-rated."

For the next ten minutes, I filled him in on the events he'd missed yesterday. Gaspar had served in the Army. His background was similar to Reacher's in some ways. He would have been an asset on the scene. He thought like Reacher would, which I'd learned to harness as a tactical advantage, too.

When I'd finished, Gaspar said, "What was your impression of Tony Clifton?"

"Sounds like you have an opinion."

He shrugged. "I know the guy. He was always, shall we say, a favorite with the ladies. Don't tell me you didn't notice. You notice everything."

"He seemed serious enough to me when he offered to help us with General Clifton." No way would I be discussing my personal reactions to Major Clifton with Gaspar. Not now. Not ever.

He remained quiet for a few minutes, thinking things through in his own way, I assumed.

The area around the Nashville airport was similar to other major civilian airports. Good roads, parking lots and garages, gas stations, hotels, and car rental joints. Nothing special. Gaspar kept his eyes on the road as we merged onto the Interstate amid heavier traffic than I'd expected for midday.

"What you need to keep in mind about the Army," he said then, "is that they take care of themselves first. Reacher is a distant memory to those guys."

True enough. "Whatever Reacher was involved in back then, it's long forgotten," I said. "Which means none of the current officers will care about it at all, even if they do remember."

He nodded. "Or, less likely, bringing old Reacher history up now will be bad news for whoever was involved. Which means watch your back."

What was important to our assignment probably didn't matter to anyone else, but we were stuck on this well-worn track. The only records we had access to on Reacher were his old Army files. Everything else that should have been in government files and public records had been deleted or hidden. We'd been warned to stop snooping into all the places where newer files should have been. We had tried anyway. So far, no dice.

Gaspar said, "We'll know soon enough whether the Clifton brothers are friend or enemy."

"Agreed." If Tony Clifton investigated the possible connections between Summer's death and *The Lucky Bar* shooting and Reacher's activities at Fort Bird, he would find something. We'd know which side Tony Clifton was on after he found the connection.

Of course, we would find the connections first. We had to.

Gaspar said, "Matthew Clifton would have been around when Jack Reacher's 1990 case was unraveling. He's two years older than Reacher, so he'd likely have been higher up the food chain, too."

We'd finally moved far enough from the airport to see some

daylight between vehicles. Gaspar set the Crown Vic's cruise control and leaned back to stretch his right leg. He drove along the Interstate at a steady five miles an hour above the speed limit.

Once he'd settled in, he said, "Joe was already at Treasury late in 1989, according to the Boss's file. But he and Jack spent a lot of time with each other around the time of Reacher's Fort Bird misadventures, flying back and forth to their mother as she was dying. Tony said his brother Matthew and Joe were still friends at that point, right? So it's possible both might have known what Jack was involved in."

My gut said both Cliftons knew a hell of a lot more than we did. "What do you think about Lesley Browning?"

Gaspar shrugged again. Which was his all-purpose gesture for answering most questions. In this case, I interpreted him to mean the trip to Nashville was a waste of time, but also an item we needed to check off our list.

"The key is Colonel Eunice Summer," he said. "Who wanted her dead? And why?"

So Gaspar's take on the noncoincidence factor between my arrival at Fort Bird to ask about Reacher and the crash—and maybe *The Lucky Bar* incident—was the same as mine. My stomach clenched and I nodded.

We'd only been partners for a short time, but hunting Jack Reacher had already proved deadly several times over. Everywhere we went, old bodies surfaced and new bodies fell, and each time Reacher was at the center. The guy was a trouble magnet. Or a trouble starter. The jury was still out on that, in my mind.

Either way, we weren't foolish enough to assume any of the Fort Bird and New Haven incidents were unrelated to Reacher.

Otherwise, the Boss wouldn't have bothered to send us there at all.

"We need to concentrate on the *how* of it," I said. "Because unless Summer was either suicidal or incredibly unlucky, the crash was staged. And staging that crash required insider information about Summer and cooperation from at least the lead big rig driver." I closed my eyes to visualize the snowy accident scene again as it had looked when I drove past on my way from the Grand Lodge to the Charlotte airport.

The section of highway at mile marker #224 was the most treacherous pavement for ten miles on either side of the crash site. Which just happened to be the stretch between the truck stop, *The Lucky Bar*, and the Fort Bird exit.

Everybody who drove that route regularly would have known the danger. Which would've included the two big rig drivers as well as Colonel Summer. One problem was that Summer had made no secret of her trip to Bird and the reason she was coming. She was investigating corruption, she'd said. Which was her normal, daily job. Tacking on the interview with me seemed like an afterthought.

"Orchestrating that crash would've taken the precision of a big-budget Hollywood production's stunt team. But it's true that only one person died. One vehicle between the two rigs. No collateral damage." Gaspar nodded as he worked through the steps I'd already trod. "That's a little too convenient. Finding out how it was done might lead us to the motive and the Machiavelli at the helm."

When he'd caught up to my logic on those points, I asked my question again. "So what *do* you think about Lesley Browning?"

He glanced at me and cocked his head. "Seems like Tony

Clifton definitely wanted us to talk to her. She must know something that we don't."

"Who doesn't?" I shrugged. "But what does she know that's important to us? And why does Tony Clifton want us to find out?"

CHAPTER SIXTEEN

GASPAR FROWNED AND RAN his fingers through his hair. "Hell, I don't know. I'm a cop, not a mind reader. You tell me what smiling Tony is up to with us."

One of us needed to go into the interview with an open mind, so I didn't answer. "Here's our exit. We're about ten minutes away."

Gaspar tapped the brake to release the cruise control and floated the Crown Vic into the exit lane as it slowed. At the bottom of the ramp was the usual cluster of gas stations and fast food joints. Gaspar pulled into one of the burger places and parked. He held up his left hand, palm flat like a traffic cop. "I know you want me to be completely comfortable."

"You bet, Chico." A bathroom-and-coffee break seemed like a good idea to me as well. "Meet you back here in a few."

He turned off the engine and locked the car as we walked toward the building. His limp was more pronounced until he walked it out, as always after an extended period of sitting. We peeled apart and took care of business.

I returned to the car first. He was a few minutes longer. He'd probably stopped to call Marie while I stood outside shaking in the cold, which was more than reasonable. But again, I wondered what was going on besides the new baby. Right now, we had plenty to worry about, so I let it go.

When he arrived with the keys and unlocked the Crown Vic, I noticed the Boss's cell phones resting inside their envelopes in the back seat. Which reminded me of the flat manila envelope. I popped the trunk, hustled around back, retrieved the flat one, slammed the trunk lid, and returned to the front seat.

Gaspar raised both eyebrows. "What is that?"

"Not sure. The soldier at the Fort Bird gate yesterday handed it to me when I turned in my visitor pass on the way out." I showed the envelope to him. "Maybe something from the Boss. Haven't had a chance to open it." That earned a puzzled look from him, but he let it pass.

My name had been hand printed on the front along with my title in all capital letters. The sort of generic printing you'd find on any field report. FBI SPECIAL AGENT KIM L. OTTO

I held out my left palm. "Hand me your pocket knife."

Gaspar fished into his right front pocket and pulled out the small jackknife that lived on his key ring.

I opened the two-inch blade and used it to slit the envelope's bottom edge, leaving the top edge undisturbed. I closed the knife and handed it back. It was a long shot, but there could've been DNA on the seal.

One palm on each edge, I pushed the envelope to widen it. Inside was a single sheet of paper, which might yield forensic evidence later, but probably wouldn't.

Without pulling the sheet out—I'd wait for that until I could document the envelope and preserve potential forensics, just in case—I could see that, printed on the front side of the paper, was a color photograph of Summer's fatal crash. The scene was recognizable despite poor print quality. I'd seen similar images at least a dozen times since yesterday, from a variety of angles and sources. My first glimpse had been news video on the big-screen TV in the lobby of the New Haven Grand Lodge, although I hadn't known Summer was involved in the crash then. After Tony Clifton had told me about Summer, I'd downloaded several TV reports to my laptop and watched them on the plane.

The panoramic image in this photograph was distinctive, though. It had been snapped by a drone or satellite camera. The shot captured the area surrounding mile marker #224, including both big rigs, and what had once been Colonel Summer's jaunty red sports car.

It took me several long seconds to realize that the crash had happened mere moments before the photo was taken, as Summer's car was a mangled mess, but both tractor drivers were still seated in their cabs.

I flipped the envelope over. With more manipulation, I could see the back of the photo paper. The same block printing had been used. 19 NOVEMBER 09:53. The exact time of the crash.

I let the envelope flatten again and handed it to Gaspar.

He examined the front, back, and self-sticking seal. He frowned when he saw the image. His frown deepened when he saw the printing on the back. He had studied both sides of the photo for a good long time before he returned the envelope to me.

"There must be millions of envelopes exactly like that at Fort Bird. Government buys them by the truckload. Nothing traceable about it as far as I can see. And that handwriting is about as generic as handwriting can be."

I popped the trunk, released the seatbelt and returned the

envelope to a secure location in my bag where it would not be damaged or discovered until we had the opportunity to inspect further.

When I returned to the front seat and settled in again, Gaspar said, "That warning is the kind of thing the Boss would do. He couldn't talk to you on a secure line because your phone was gone. He'd have wanted to send you a warning."

"Maybe." The Boss's motives were never that pure. He had a hidden agenda. We were all involved in a high-stakes chess match in which he was the king and we were pawns. He'd made it abundantly clear that he intended to win and he was willing to sacrifice both Gaspar and me to do it. "How do you feel about Tony Clifton now?"

"He could have managed to deliver that envelope, sure." Gaspar nodded slowly. "If he did, it means he'd have known Summer was already dead the whole time. When he was talking to you, in his office and all the way through lunch. And he never said anything."

"That would make him a pretty cold bastard, don't you think?" The hair on the back of my neck was tingling, but I'd felt nothing of the kind when he was alone with me in my hotel room. At least, I didn't remember feeling the least bit apprehensive. "Chatting with me, flirting with female officers, laughing with his colleagues. Offering to help. Telling me stories about Joe Reacher teaching him chess."

I stopped for breath and considered the idea. "And all the time, he knew Summer was dead?"

"Every soldier is a trained killer, Sunshine. Most of us get in, do the job, and get out. But trust me when I tell you that it takes a certain kind of emotional detachment to excel at that particular skillset for a couple of decades." Gaspar had started the Crown

Vic and flipped the heat on, but the transmission was still firmly in Park. His full attention was on the subject. "These days, the Army's a lot smaller. More and better candidates for fewer officer slots."

I nodded. Modern warfare was long on technology and shorter on human hands. And about to get even shorter. A big argument was going on in Washington right now about budget cuts and forced reductions again. The politicians were adamant about defense spending cuts and the Pentagon objected to being forced to do more with less. The battle seemed endless.

Gaspar rolled his shoulders and stretched his right leg again. "Which means these days that only two kinds of soldiers get promoted as far up the ladder as Matt and Tony Clifton. The really good ones, and the ones that are very well connected."

"Or both really good *and* well connected." I rubbed the back of my neck, thinking through the exact sequence of events from the time I got the order to interview Summer from the Boss though my exit from Fort Bird. "Threatening a guy well-connected and very skilled like that could be a quick way to an early grave."

"We're late. We've got to go." Gaspar moved the big tank's transmission into drive and rolled slowly toward Pine Street. He turned right, following the GPS directions to Woodland Estates, while we both sat with our own vibes, as my mother would say.

CHAPTER SEVENTEEN

LESLEY BROWNING'S BIO SAID she lived here with her husband and two high school-aged kids. She'd been married only once after Joe Reacher. The second marriage had produced the kids.

Twin girls, aged fifteen. Based on photos, they were the image of what their mother must have looked like back when Joe knew her. Which is to say cute, freckled, friendly. Not sexy or beautiful in any conventional way. More like wholesome, trustworthy, and reliable.

Which told me more about young Joe Reacher than a complete set of encyclopedia-length background checks. But Joe Reacher was dead and not our assignment.

Was there anything to be gleaned from Lesley Browning about Joe's brother Jack?

Some brothers were as different as night and day. They looked different, pursued divergent careers, even communicated like strangers sometimes. The Reacher brothers might have been like that.

Based on their Army headshots, though, Joe and Jack

Reacher were like my own three brothers. Which is to say they could have been clones. And DNA is destiny. But a tiny variance in one of those genes could make a whale of a difference.

Both Reachers were big and fair with blue eyes and broad shoulders. They were military brats. Born on the other side of the world and raised on bases around the globe.

They could have been glued together or wedged apart by those experiences. Joe was older and entered West Point first, and Jack, like younger brothers everywhere, followed. Similarities could have ended there. Or not.

Maybe we'd get lucky with Lesley Browning. This interview could be the break we needed to finally make some progress. I hoped.

Woodland Estates was a well-established neighborhood. The homes were enormous by my Detroit area standards. Brick construction, multiple rooflines, four-car garages, wide lots with plenty of grass. Perfect asphalt pavement curved through the neighborhood abutted by unblemished cement curbs. Flat sidewalks beribboned the lush green lawns and what was left of the flowering annuals.

Either Lesley Browning and her family were well beyond upwardly mobile, dwelling within firmly settled one-percenters, or the cost of living in suburban Nashville was significantly below the national median. Given the strong economy here, I'd bet my government salary on the former.

Gaspar parked the Crown Vic in the circular driveway of the mini-mansion because there were no cars parked on the streets. The last thing we needed today was to be towed. We left the car and approached the double oak doors in the center of the main façade. Gaspar leaned over and rang the bell.

I expected a butler or maid or something to be standing on

the other side, but the door was opened by one of the twins. She smiled wide, revealing a mouth full of multi-colored braces.

Putting a friendly tone in my voice, I said, "I'm Kim Otto and this is Carlos Gaspar. Is your mom around?"

She shook hands with me and her smile never faltered for a second. I detected no wariness at all. "Come in. It's really cold out there." She stepped back into the foyer and pulled the door open wide.

"That would be great." I stepped into the dimly lit interior and Gaspar followed me, closing the door behind him. "We'll wait here."

For the first time, her composure faltered slightly. Perhaps she was realizing now that if we were really friends of her mother's, we would have continued the chatter and followed her into the house.

"I-I'll be right back," she said before she turned and slipped toward the back of the house. My stomach growled in response to the aroma of baking desserts wafting to my nose. It was the time of year when baked goods and party foods abounded. Thanksgiving was just around the corner. Attendance at the Otto family feast was mandatory.

The house seemed symmetrically divided on each side of the front entrance. The large open foyer was roughly the size of my entire Detroit apartment. A wide staircase curved up one level on the right side of the foyer. Double doors to our left and right led to rooms on either side of the entry, and straight ahead was the back of the house, where the kitchen must have been.

We waited two full minutes for Lesley Browning, long enough that I began to wonder whether she was home after all. But she emerged with a flour smudge on her nose, wearing an apron, and drying her hands on a kitchen towel. She began talking as she approached.

"I'm so sorry to have kept you waiting. Katie said you were here and I thought she would just bring you back." By the time she stopped walking and talking, she was close enough that I could see her freckles. She reached out for a firm handshake just as her daughter had. "You work with my husband, right? He said you'd be later, so I'm sorry that I'm not quite ready."

"Ma'am, I'm FBI Special Agent Kim Otto." I reached into my jacket and showed her my badge wallet. Gaspar did the same. "This is Special Agent Carlos Gaspar. Is there somewhere we can have a private conversation?"

Most people are at least wary when FBI agents invade, and those that aren't can be suspicious or downright hostile. Lesley Browning acted like an FBI visit to her home was no more unusual than a visit from the Avon lady. "Sure, let's go in here."

She led us toward the double entry doors on the left and we walked into a traditionally decorated formal living room full of ball-and-claw feet and Queen Anne legs and brocade upholstery and dense blocks of mahogany case goods.

She gestured to a loveseat, closed the doors and sat across from us in the center of an identical loveseat. Every inch the fit, smiling contemporary housewife, she looked like an anachronism amid the rather staid traditional furnishings. "How can I help you?"

I felt like I had landed in an alternate universe again. No one but my father had ever greeted me with that much warmth. Either Gaspar felt the same or he was simply waiting for me to take the lead.

"Thank you for seeing us." I blinked a few times to clear my head. "You are Lesley Browning, aren't you?"

Her smile wrinkled the freckles on her nose and reached all the way to her very friendly eyes. "Oh my gosh, no one has called me that in years. But yes, my maiden name was Lesley Browning. Why do you ask?"

Maiden name? The bio we'd located indicated no name change. "Bear with me a moment, ma'am, just to be sure that we have the right person. Did you once live at 7683 Jackson Street in Newburgh, New York?"

"I lived there from the time I was born until college." Her smile never faltered and she nodded. "Why?"

I gave her my standard explanation of our mission. It was close enough to the truth to pass without objection. "We prepare background checks on people who are being considered for special government employment. It may seem exceptionally thorough to go back as far as college, but..." I let my voice fall away and shrugged as if to say I was just doing my job and hoped she'd help me out.

"Okay." She nodded enthusiastically and clasped her hands in her lap. "How can I help?"

Good question.

CHAPTER EIGHTEEN

INVOKING THE NAME "REACHER" was always the tricky part. Reactions from prior witnesses at this point had ranged from denial to horror to tears to physical pushback. I braced for anything and opened my mouth and, at the last possible moment, vectored to a tangent. "We're interested in speaking with you about Joe Reacher."

Her eyes widened, and her mouth formed a little "O" and she drew in the tiniest gasp. Then her smile returned, wider this time, along with her composure. "I haven't heard that name in a very long time, either. How is Joe? Where is he now? I would love to see him again."

Gaspar must have missed my intention. He interrupted. "Kim, you misspoke. You said Joe Reacher was being considered for the job, but the candidate is Jack Reacher."

"Did I?" I cocked my head and frowned a little and resisted the urge to glare at him. "I'm sorry. It's been a long day. Carlos is right. I meant to say it's Jack Reacher who is being considered for the job, not Joe Reacher." I shrugged and offered an apologetic smile. "Their names are so similar and I've never met either of them."

"Don't worry. I understand. They were somewhat interchangeable to me, too. They looked a lot alike. If you met one brother in the dark, you could easily believe he was the other one. And their names are similar though of course everyone called Jack 'Reacher.' I asked Joe why once, and he said that's just the way it always was. Even their mother called him 'Reacher.'" She gave a little laugh. "I really can't imagine that, can you? Why would she have started doing that?"

I shrugged as though I couldn't say. Because it was news to me. Interesting to hear that the brothers were almost interchangeable in appearance. I wondered if that was what got Joe Reacher killed. Had Jack been the intended victim? I put that question on my mental checklist for later.

"Anyway, the two of them were very close. They'd never been separated until Joe went to West Point. Two years later, when Jack joined Joe there, they hung out together often. It would be easy to get them confused."

"So, Jack Reacher, then," I said, settling in and smiling as if we were girlfriends about to dish. "Let's start with when you knew him and how."

She moved deeper into the loveseat and relaxed a little more. She tilted her head back and took a breath as if she were thinking about a long ago experience that she enjoyed very much. Maybe she was.

"I was eighteen, but I guess I was still a senior in high school when I first met Joe. He was at West Point with a neighborhood boy, Matthew Clifton." Her tone was wistful, pleasant. "And then I met Jack later. When I went to West Point to see Joe."

"You and Joe must have been good friends." I nodded like an understanding girlfriend would do.

"Oh! I thought you knew." She laughed. The sound was light, easy. Not the least bit guarded. "Joe was my first love. He and I were married. It only lasted less than six months. But we stayed friends after that."

I arched my eyebrows and widened my eyes. "I see."

"I was too young and my parents were opposed. Of course, at the time, I thought they were being so unreasonable." She laughed again. "But when Joe graduated West Point, he planned to serve in the Army and then move on to another agency. Well, even back then I knew I didn't want to be an Army wife. I would never have been any good at that. Joe was disappointed. He was the kind of guy who committed himself to everything and never gave up when there were problems, you know?"

"So you divorced?" Gaspar asked.

"Well, we got married because I was pregnant and Joe insisted he had to take care of me. Joe was like that. He always wanted to take care of everybody." She cocked her head and seemed to be thinking about that time. She frowned a little and took a deep breath. "And after my miscarriage, I guess a lot of things just hit home to me. I was too young to be a mother then and once the baby was gone…. It just gave me a chance to reconsider, I guess."

Gaspar's spine straightened. "What about Joe? How did he feel about all of this?" His tone bore heavy disapproval. He'd be gutted if Marie left him or if he lost his kids. He might not survive it.

Lesley must have sensed his meaning because she dropped her gaze and took another deep breath before she raised it again. "I don't think Joe was ready to be a father, either. He said he was ready and I was proud of him for wanting to take care of me and the baby." She paused a couple of beats. "We were too young. At least, I was. But we stayed friends for a long time. Joe called occasionally. Cards at birthdays and holidays, you know." She paused and then, wistful again, repeated herself: "I would like to see him again."

I let that comment pass because I didn't want to get into any conversation about how Joe Reacher died on a lonely road in the middle of nowhere fifteen years ago. Nor did I want to deal with her reactions. Instead, I asked, "And Jack Reacher? What can you tell us about him?"

She smiled again, livelier now. "Reacher was a whole different kettle of fish."

"How is that?" Gaspar phrased it like he really wanted to know.

"He was smart like Joe. He was a whiz with numbers. And he had an amazing ability to know the time, even though he never wore a watch. Like a savant or something. He didn't talk much. The strong, silent type, I guess. He did well in school, too. But his skills were well, shall we say more physical in nature?" Her grin widened. Probably remembering some sort of trouble Jack had started or finished. "When he went straight into the Army and joined the MPs, I know Joe felt Reacher had made the right choice. Joe said if I was ever in trouble, I should call Reacher because he would always do what he believed was the right thing."

"And Joe wasn't as physical as Jack?" Because Joe was Army all the way. He had served in Military Intelligence. A soft-hearted man would never have made those choices in the first place. And he'd have washed out early if he'd mistakenly done so, instead of developing Joe Reacher's impressive record.

She laughed. "Oh, Joe was no weenie or anything. He was as tough as any guy. Sometimes a little too quick to square off when he was pushed. Sometimes he shoved back a little too hard. Sure."

As I suspected. I nodded to encourage her, but she didn't elaborate.

Gaspar asked, "When was the last time you saw either Jack or Joe Reacher?"

"For Joe, let me see." Lesley looked at the ceiling a moment, considering. "It was a couple of years after Josephine died. Their mother."

"Did you know her?" I asked.

"Not really. I never met her, actually." Lesley shook her head. "She was briefly my mother-in-law and she was over the moon when she learned I was pregnant, Joe said. I talked to her on the phone a couple of times. She had a lovely French accent. I liked her and I think she never forgave me for divorcing Joe."

"What makes you say that?"

"Oh, Joe all but said as much. As I said, we stayed in touch for a time. That woman was tough as nails. Her own marriage wasn't the easiest, so she felt I gave up too soon and too easily. I think Joe was her favorite of the two boys, although she certainly loved them both and they loved her too. Joe said she was the glue that held their family together." She paused again, lost in a memory. "He called me when he found out she had terminal cancer. He was very upset about it, but he said Reacher was taking it too stoically."

I cocked my head. "What did he mean by that?" The emerging picture she was painting of Jack Reacher was fascinatingly different from what I'd heard from every source before. Different, too, from his Army record, which was all I had to go on. Maybe the years had changed him, as Master Sergeant Jones had said back at Fort Bird yesterday, but not for the better.

"Joe always said he had to look after Reacher, but he said Reacher has the strength of two men and thinks he's the one who protects Joe. Once Joe told me that if anything ever happened to him, he didn't know what Reacher would do. I'm sure Reacher felt at least that strongly about Josephine. I know Joe did." She opened her hands and rested one on each knee. "Like I said, those boys were very close. Two peas in a pod. Josephine died a few days after that and Joe called to tell me about the funeral. I wanted to go, but it was in Paris. That's where she lived."

"And Jack," I said. "When did you last see him?"

"I don't know." She cocked her head again and thought about it a while. "Maybe five years ago?" That set my body humming like a tuning fork. If Lesley noticed my reaction, she didn't let on. "It was after he left the Army because I remember telling him how shocked I was. The Army had seemed such a perfect fit for him, you know? He was really well suited to the work."

"So. About five years ago, where did you see him?"

"I was at a conference with my husband in East L.A. It was the strangest thing because I saw Reacher on the street. He was older, but otherwise just the same as I remembered. Huge. Fit. Hands the size of baseball mitts. He picked me up and hugged me tight and I thought I wasn't going to be able to breathe ever again." She laughed briefly at the memory and then she frowned. "He looked like a hobo, though. He was wearing civilian clothes that didn't fit him very well like he'd bought them off the rack at a farm goods store or something. Terrible haircut. I thought maybe he was having financial problems."

"Did you ask him about that?" Gaspar's ears perked up. Financial problems could and often did lead to crime.

"Well, no. That would have been rude, don't you think?" She glanced at Gaspar and paused. She frowned in concentration. "He was meeting old Army friends, he said. We didn't talk long. I'm sorry I didn't spend more time with him that day, though because I never saw him again."

"Did he give you a card or an address?"

It was an odd question to ask since we'd told her he applied for a job. Not many people would be considered for a sensitive government job without a permanent residence. But she didn't hesitate before she replied. "I'm afraid not."

"You've been very helpful, Ma'am," Gaspar said. "We've taken up enough of your time." He stood and buttoned his jacket. "But if we need anything more, can we contact you again?"

"Of course. Please give my best to Reacher and Joe. And tell them to come by." She stood and straightened the wrinkles from her slacks, then smiled at us each in turn. "I'd love to catch up with them both."

She walked us to the front door.

"This is a lovely home you have here," Gaspar said, looking around. "What kind of work does your husband do?"

"Thomas? He's a defense contractor. Years ago, he was in the Army before we married. JAG Corps. Now his company produces unmanned tank systems and drones for the military."

Gaspar pushed his hands into his pockets. "Thomas's last name is what, again?"

"Same as mine now. O'Connor."

"How did you meet him?"

"I have Joe Reacher to thank for that, too. After Joe and I divorced, I thought I'd never fall in love again. And I didn't, for years." She smiled again and brushed her hair away from her face. She opened the door and the cold air rushed inside. "But Joe and I stayed friends and in one of those quirky twists of fate, Joe was the one who introduced me to Thomas. Now I have Thomas and the girls and it's all worked out. Everything always does, don't you think?"

CHAPTER NINETEEN

WE GOT INTO THE Crown Vic and headed back the way we came. We sat with our thoughts for a while. He halfway wasn't much of a small talker, which suited me fine. About back to the Nashville airport, he said, "Are you going to call or should I?"

He meant that one of us was going to have to open the padded envelopes in the back seat and fire up the Boss's cell phones. The phones were tracking us now, no doubt. But if I wanted an appointment with General Matthew Clifton on the base at Fort Herald in Dallas—and if I didn't before, I certainly did now—I'd need some heavy-duty help to make that happen.

The Boss could easily pave the way if he was so inclined. The FBI can go just about anywhere these days. And Gaspar was an Army veteran with a veteran's card, which sometimes allowed him access to military installations without prior notice, depending on the threat level each day. But it made no sense to travel all the way to Dallas before solving the administrative issues.

The other option was to accept Major Tony Clifton's offer to intercede with his brother for us. Gaspar's question meant that he had considered Tony as an option and rejected it.

"There's an exit up ahead. Let's stop for coffee," I replied, which was a way to let him know I wanted to discuss the options away from the Boss's ears and before we went any further.

Gaspar glanced at me and returned his gaze to the road. "Whatever you say."

We never assumed we were truly under the radar. Usually, someone was watching and listening and manipulating. Usually, that was the Boss, but other eyes and ears were on us, too. Some of them, we were by now well convinced, were connected to Reacher. When we wanted privacy, evasive maneuvers were required.

Listening to conversations in the open air is doable, but it's harder than monitoring inside a vehicle. Roadside restaurants are typically busy. There would be lots of conflicting cell phone traffic. It was complicated to isolate particular conversations amid dozens of others and it required extra time, more equipment. Which gave us small windows of privacy when we could manage to immerse ourselves in crowds.

At the next exit, Gaspar chose a parking lot surrounded by a clump of restaurants, gas stations and a strip mall knotted together by concrete. He parked the Crown Vic in one of the lot's busier areas. We left our personal cell phones in the car, too, and walked fifty yards away before either of us spoke again.

Gaspar's limp slowed us down, but we weren't headed anywhere in particular so it didn't matter. He had popped at least two Tylenol already when he thought I wasn't looking.

"We can agree that Tony Clifton sent us to Lesley Browning for a reason." His voice held a question although the words did not. "Did you hear the reason from her?"

"Not exactly. But the connection is there," I said. "Jack and Joe Reacher and Joe's ex, Lesley Browning, were all connected to General Matthew and Major Tony Clifton because they were all friends. They lived in the same neighborhood and the four men went to West Point. Colonel Summer was connected to Jack Reacher and Tony Clifton because she worked with them both."

"Summer was connected to Matthew Clifton, too. Because she'd worked with him prosecuting the events in the old JAG report, if nothing else. Senior officers are a small and exclusive club. They all know each other."

I smiled. He really was beginning to understand how I think. Which was a little scary, but more convenient than having to explain all the time. "And how about Lesley's husband?"

He gave me the side-eye. "Possible. We know Thomas O'Connor signed off on that old corruption case as the junior JAG with Matthew Clifton. But he's been out of the Army for a long time."

"Chico, in my book, being a defense contractor is *not* being out of the Army." He raised an eyebrow. "The Army is his one and only customer. You've never worked as a civilian and I have. I'm here to tell you, customers are king."

We walked and he thought about it a bit. "Let's say you're right. Where are you going with this?"

I'd been hunched into my blazer and now took a deep breath and stretched the tension from my shoulders. "I think I'm still going to Fort Herald. But the question is whether we should go to O'Connor's office before or after."

"Cuts down on the plane travel if we do it now."

"Exactly."

"Are you going to tell him?" He meant the Boss.

"He already knows. The question is why he wants us to interview O'Connor. What he wants us to find out that he doesn't already know."

We turned and walked back toward the car.

"You get the coffee and I'll make the call," Gaspar said.

"10-4," I replied and he grinned.

I chose the busiest of the fast food joints and the longest line waiting to order.

Gaspar could bring the Boss up to speed. I had no intention of joining any conversation with him just yet. The man was using me as a gun dog to serve some purpose he refused to disclose. More than once, his secrets had almost gotten me killed, and Gaspar too. He showed zero remorse for that and zero interest in changing the dynamic. Which meant I had zero interest in chatting with him except when communication was essential.

I ran the events through my head again. Somehow Jack Reacher was at the center of this thing, whatever the thing actually was. He had not been to Fort Bird since 1990. Yet, one or more of his actions in the few days he was there had caused ripples like dropping a stone into an ocean. Only Reacher's effect was more like dropping a boulder into a puddle.

Motives for murder were not much debated in law enforcement circles. The FBI manual limited the options to four classes and a bunch of sub-classifications, but they boiled down to six motives: profit, revenge, jealousy, to conceal a crime, to avoid humiliation or disgrace, and homicidal mania. In the case of *The Lucky Bar* shooter, homicidal mania was the clear favorite. But it didn't sit right with me. And the motive for killing Summer? Could have been any of the others.

My turn at the register finally came. I ordered black coffee for me and coffee with a quart of cream and half a cup of sugar for Gaspar. I added a couple of fried apple pies and paid the bill and carried the paper bag toward the Crown Vic.

The thing that I'd been worrying around in my head since *The Lucky Bar* shootout was a single question: What could Reacher have possibly done that would cause a long-dormant situation to erupt into murder all these years later?

The answer teased me like a mouse hiding in the dark. I could hear it scurrying around, but every time I turned on the light, I couldn't find it. All I saw was evidence that the mouse had been there.

CHAPTER TWENTY

WHEN I RETURNED TO the car and we'd divided the gourmet meal, Gaspar reported. "He says he'll arrange the meeting. He'll call back when it's scheduled."

I shrugged, took a bite of my apple pie, and hauled out my laptop.

After a few minutes work with the court-martial report and Internet searches, I found the information for the second JAG officer. Thomas O'Connor, Lesley's husband. His current employer was Dynamic Defense Systems, located south of Nashville. I programmed the address into the GPS and Gaspar pointed the Crown Vic in the right direction.

We had both read the old JAG court-martial report. Even on the surface, the situation was bad. Three senior officers convicted of crimes serious enough to have carried the death penalty.

"Only fourteen crimes carry the death penalty under the Uniform Code of Military Justice. At the senior officer level, crimes like that are rare," I said, dusting off and donning my lawyer hat briefly.

"I checked," Gaspar said. "We've got only five convicted servicemen awaiting execution now, out of all the military branches. All five were guilty of premeditated murder or felony murder."

"Right. But none of those five were officers. And no convicted serviceman has been executed since 1961."

Gaspar glanced over at me. "So you think that Reacher was in charge of the investigation that led to the prosecutions in the JAG report? Or he was involved in the crimes and got himself busted instead of prosecuted?"

I nodded. "Which one do you put your money on?"

"I don't see them letting an MP Major like Reacher avoid Leavenworth with the others if he was involved with the same crimes."

"Why not?"

"Because they prosecuted the bigger fish. Why would they let the smaller one go?"

I had my theories on that, but my gut said Gaspar was right. Reacher's crimes were different in kind and degree from the officers who were prosecuted. "Summer was his number two on the case. Fairly chivalrous of him to let her take the credit for the bust, don't you think?"

"I figure it was the times. The Army was on the cusp of some major downsizing right then." He shrugged. "She was probably at the decision point. Go, or stay. If she got promoted, she'd stay."

"The names of the officers were redacted from the JAG report." I closed the laptop. "But if you were looking for the names, how would you find out who they were?"

"The paperwork would tell you if you had the time and the energy to sort through it. There weren't that many officers on either the infantry or the armored side, even back then." He drained his coffee and tossed the empty cup over his shoulder into the back. When we turned in the car, there'd be a pile of trash back there. "You could get lists of all the officers and trace what happened to each one around that timeframe. It wouldn't take long to find the right names by the process of elimination."

I nodded. It was the kind of grunt-work we had a team of people to do on normal FBI assignments. But we didn't have the luxury on this one. "Summer had been ordered to tell me everything about what happened with Reacher back then. I'm guessing that's the part that got her killed."

"Because she knew things she had not revealed before?"

I nodded again. "And because someone else was aware of what Summer had previously kept out of the files."

"What we need to find, then, are the others who knew what Summer knew."

"As the first step. The second step is to find out why they didn't want her to tell me."

"And Lesley Browning's husband can help with the first step?"

"He might be able to help with both. JAG officers are lawyers. Lawyers usually come in after the fact. Whatever Summer told Matthew Clifton and O'Connor about Reacher at the time should have become part of the report." I paused. "And it's not there. At least, it's not in the unredacted portions we've been allowed to read."

"So you think O'Connor wasn't involved in the original incidents, but he knew what they were and he knew the underlying facts. And he kept them buried." Gaspar nodded as he worked things through. "That tracks."

"He knew at least enough of the facts to secure the

confessions from the three officers and put the matter to bed quietly without airing dirty laundry in public at a sensitive time in Army history."

"It's Army SOP," Gaspar said. "Keeping things on the down low would have been at least as important as exacting justice for the underlying crime."

Which was the problem. Summer had died a colonel. She'd made her career on the old case, sure. But she must have performed well afterward to continue advancing.

On paper, she seemed worthy enough. No record of disciplinary action that I'd found. She would want to protect the Army's reputation from what happened back then, and her own reputation, too. In fact, she'd have wanted to keep all of her investigations under the radar, which was very hard to do in the information age.

"Why kill her now?" I asked.

He shrugged, his all-purpose response.

The GPS led us directly to Dynamic Defense Systems after about twenty minutes' driving time. The building was a five-story mirrored cube. Reflective coated glass, they called it. Energy efficient because it reflected the heat in the summertime. Office towers in Sunbelt states like this one were uninhabitable without it.

The cubed building was almost invisible. Trees planted around the cube were reflected, too. It seemed like a small forest sitting amid the asphalt instead of a building full of classified government secret weapon systems.

At the front gate, Gaspar showed his badge. "FBI Special Agents. We're here to see Thomas O'Connor."

The guard made a phone call, prepared two visitor passes and directed us to park in the visitor parking area near the front entrance. The lot was packed. Gaspar found an empty slot at the end of the row.

We parked and entered through double glass doors that parted in the center automatically like a supermarket's. Except these also probably performed a full body scan of every visitor on the way in and on the way out.

The floor inside was carpeted and probably laced with tracking grids that gathered biometrics like weight and shoe size from which height and sex were extrapolated and matched with the body scans.

Leather chairs and tables seemed carelessly tossed around the lobby. A square reception desk that echoed the building's exterior design squatted in the center of the room. A youngish woman sat inside the square. She looked like Dolly Parton's granddaughter. This was Nashville so she might have been an aspiring country singer, too.

Gaspar gave our names. Five minutes later, a professionally dressed woman in her mid-thirties entered through a door on the opposite side of the lobby and approached us.

"Agents Otto and Gaspar? I'm Delphina Osgood, Mr. O'Connor's assistant. Please come with me."

We followed her through a labyrinth of corridors that smelled like warm apple cider until we reached a corner office in the back. The door was open.

Thomas O'Connor, looking exactly like his corporate headshot on the web page, paced the room. He was thicker through the middle than expected, but otherwise of average size and build. Clean-shaven. Brown hair neatly parted and combed. A plain gold wedding band encircled the appropriate finger.

He held a telephone receiver to his ear and occasionally

responded with "Uh huh," and "Right," and "I see." He waved us into the room with one hand.

Delphina Osgood stood aside and said, "Would you like coffee?"

The question always jolts me. It's like asking if I would like oxygen. "That would be great. Black."

Gaspar smiled and said, "Cream and sugar, if you have it."

"Certainly," she replied and left.

The office, like the building, was neat, square, contemporary, and impersonal. And utterly ordinary. As if someone had ordered the entire setup from an online catalog in one package called "The Office." Dark wood desk and credenza. Black leather desk chair and visitor chairs. Plain beige drywall surrounded us on all the vertical surfaces. The carpet was darker beige. Framed photos on the walls were probably ordered from the same catalog.

Delphina Osgood brought the coffee and one for O'Connor and placed our business cards on his desk before she left. After muttering a few more verbal nothings into the receiver, O'Connor ended his call and turned his attention to us.

"I've already told the FBI everything I know. I thought this was over." His delivery was smooth as if he talked to the FBI on a regular basis, which it sounded like he probably did. Probably on a first name basis with every security agency in the country, public and private, too.

He sat behind the desk and folded his hands on top. He glanced at the cards. "Otto and Gaspar, is it?"

"You've already told the FBI everything you know about what?"

"The Clifton investigation. That's why you're here, right? Matthew Clifton is one of the finest men I've ever met. He wouldn't violate contracting ethics or any other kind of ethics. I don't know who your whistleblower is, but he's barking up the wrong tree here." O'Connor's earnest expression matched his words. "The Justice Department arrested and convicted Hanlon. That's the end of it."

His tone suggested the opposite. He clearly subscribed to the a-strong-offense-is-the-best-defense approach.

Fine with me. I'd circle back to the whole "Clifton investigation" business.

"Actually, we're with the Special Personnel Task Force. We are completing a background investigation on a former Army officer." Defense contractors, particularly former JAG officers, weren't the same as housewives. Unlike interviewing his wife, we didn't need to warm him up first. He wouldn't think the abrupt statement or an active investigation required further explanation. Not at first.

"Who is the candidate?"

"Major Jack Reacher. We understand you had contact with him while you were both on active duty. Have you kept in touch with Major Reacher?"

He frowned as if he was puzzled now by the name and the question. "It's a big army and I haven't been active for a long time. Can you give me a bit more to jog my memory?"

"How about Colonel Eunice Summer?"

"Yes, of course, I've worked with Colonel Summer. Small woman. Carried herself like a catwalk model." He nodded, but the frown stayed in place. "I retired eighteen years ago, and I haven't seen her much since then."

"Back in 1990, you prosecuted a case with General Matthew Clifton. Colonel Summer was the MP handling the criminal investigation. Major Jack Reacher was Summer's senior officer."

His frown cleared. "Yes. I do recall. Though Major Reacher did not assist us in the prosecution. He had been reassigned by the time I began working on the case."

"Do you know why he was reassigned?"

"Let me think a minute." He steepled his fingers together and rested his forefingers against his bottom lip. "It seems I remember something about a parking lot brawl. A complaint was filed against him by a fellow officer, as I recall. The complaint was investigated and probably substantiated, given the outcome."

"Meaning Reacher was involved in a bar fight? That wouldn't be enough to get him busted back to Captain," Gaspar said. "Had to be more to it than a brawl."

"You're right, Agent Gaspar," O'Connor replied. "It was a long time ago and I handled a lot of cases after that. I'm sorry I can't remember the specifics. Maybe there was a civilian involved? That would make sense."

"You never interviewed Reacher in your big case against the senior officers?"

"We didn't need to. The officers confessed, I believe. And we had Lieutenant Summer, who was familiar with all the facts."

"Did you ever have any dealings with Reacher after that?"

He shook his head slowly as if he was thinking about it and coming up with nothing. "I'm pretty sure I never crossed paths with him at all, back then or since."

"What's your job here?" I asked.

"I'm the Chief Compliance Officer. I make sure that we comply with all federal rules and regulations. You wouldn't believe the paperwork involved in an operation like this." He laughed and then seemed to remember he was talking to the FBI. "Or maybe you would."

"What exactly is your firm's work with the Army?"

"Design, development, and manufacture of advanced weapons systems. Without revealing any secrets, we are involved with what they call The Big Power War."

"What does that mean?"

"It means we anticipate a conflict with other major powers instead of the ragtag guerrillas and insurgents we have been fighting in Iraq and Afghanistan. The change in focus requires a return to conventional warfare equipment, such as tanks and bombers."

"And that's where Dynamic Defense Systems comes in."

"Exactly. We're not the only company providing newer and better equipment, but we are one of the bigger, more successful contractors."

"And how are you working with Colonel Summer?"

"We're not. I haven't actually worked with Colonel Summer directly since that case all those years ago." He stood, which suggested we should do the same. He gestured with an extended arm and open palm toward the door. "I'm sorry I can't be of help to you. If you think of anything else, call me anytime."

Delphina Osgood reappeared as if she'd been listening for her cue. Maybe she had been.

I ignored her and took a solid guess. "Colonel Summer was handling the Clifton investigation, though. So you've been working with her on that, right?"

"That matter is not being handled by the FBI." He gave us the sweeping open palm again. "I'm not allowed to discuss military issues with civilians. You'll need to get answers on military matters directly from the Army."

He picked up a ringing phone and turned his back to us.

Gaspar shrugged. We followed Delphina Osgood, who escorted us all the way to the double glass doors that opened automatically and scanned us as we exited. To be sure we'd left the premises instead of lying in wait, or something.

Standing outside on the pavement, Gaspar said, "Well that was a total waste of time."

"You're a man, you tell me," I said, maybe a bit too belligerently. "How likely is it that Joe Reacher is O'Connor's wife's ex and the man responsible for introducing him to his beloved, yet O'Connor has to strain to remember the Reacher name? And what about that bullshit on the Clifton investigation? You buying any of that?"

Gaspar smirked. "He did display an appalling lack of curiosity, didn't he?"

CHAPTER TWENTY-ONE

AFTER SURVIVING ANOTHER FLIGHT, we reached another military base. They were all different, yet familiar. Each one popped my internal alert level into the red zone and held it there. Bases were populated with highly trained military personnel and thousands of weapons and plenty of tension. In my book, that meant a potential disaster waiting to happen at a moment's notice. Civilians who lived on base as well as those who came and went presented another layer of risk. The adrenaline running through my system could have propelled an old mare to the Triple Crown.

This time the sign said:

> WELCOME TO FORT HERALD
> HOME OF AMERICA'S ARMORED CORPS

This was the most populous U.S. military installation in the world. Its massive dimensions—350 square miles, more than 215,000 acres—could only be truly appreciated from the air. It's worth the trip to Google Maps.

We entered through the main gate and cleared the first hurdles easily because the Boss had paved the way. Our credentials were examined and we were provided with visitor passes and directions to General Matthew Clifton's office. So far, so good.

We drove less than a mile past buildings and lawns that were meant for visitors, not combat troop training. The soldiers were easy to distinguish from the civilians because soldiers were dressed in ACUs. Everyone moved with purpose.

November was warmer in Dallas than in the North Carolina Mountains or Nashville, but a chill wind still blew through the parking lot. We left the Crown Vic parked as instructed and made our way to the headquarters building, which was nowhere close to as nice as Dynamic Defense Systems. This was the Army. Strictly utilitarian, even for the upper echelons.

General Matthew Clifton was waiting for us in the Commanding Officer's assigned duty station, which he would occupy for a few more days, his brother had said. His appearance was startling because he resembled Tony not at all. He was of average height, with a receding hairline and sandy hair. The only physical attribute they shared was a pair of striking bottle-green eyes.

Nothing about him was sparkling or friendly. Certainly, he sported no blinding mega-watt smile. His style was all business. "Cooper and Finlay asked me to hear you out. I have ten minutes, so let's get to it."

Both names jarred. Charles Cooper was a name rarely uttered by friend or foe on this assignment. I didn't even *think* about him by name, and Gaspar and I certainly never used the Boss's name, either. Not even between us. We were under the radar. He didn't want his fingerprints all over our work. He'd made that crystal clear from the outset.

But *Finlay*, too? Another name I didn't expect to encounter here, for sure. Lamont Finlay, Ph.D. Special Assistant to the President for Strategy. One of the most powerful men on the planet. *Why the hell was he involved in this?*

General Clifton thought I already knew. Which meant I couldn't ask him outright.

So I did as he'd instructed and went straight to the meat. "Yesterday, three unusual things occurred at Fort Bird. All three are related to an old case handled by Jack Reacher's 110th Special Investigations Unit back in 1990. A case you were involved with, too. We are trying to figure out whether Reacher is connected to these new crimes, or if someone with an old grievance is fighting back. Maybe trying to frame them or exact some kind of revenge. Or both."

Clifton barely blinked. He pulled his jacket off the back of his chair and slipped his arms into first one sleeve and then another. "How does any of this involve me?"

"You knew both Jack and Joe Reacher, I'm told."

"What's your point?"

"My point, General, is that the junior officer Reacher worked with on that 1990 case is now dead, and your brother has Reacher's former XO position. You were the senior JAG officer who prosecuted the case Reacher handled, and you are currently doing business with the junior JAG officer who prosecuted it along with you. And if that's not enough, that same junior JAG officer is married to Joe Reacher's ex-wife. That is a truly remarkable tangle of connections."

"You could connect every Army officer who's served over the last twenty-five years with three phone calls. Every top-level government civilian connected to the military, too, if you wanted to." He shrugged and buttoned his jacket. "I fail to see the relevance of any of this. Why are Cooper and Finlay interested in Reacher after all this time?"

"I can't speak for them," I said. But what I thought was, *Good question.* "I need to know what went down back then. And whether Reacher or someone else is delivering payback."

"Cooper and Finlay know all of this already. Reacher did a lot of things right, but he was no saint. He was busted back to captain because he's got some kind of god complex. He decided to be judge, jury, and executioner all rolled into some kind of avenging angel." He collected his briefcase. "He was wrong. People didn't like it."

"People?"

"The politicians. The politically correct crowd. People who think what we do here is some kind of goddamned John Wayne movie."

"Okay, General," Gaspar said. "But what did he do? Exactly."

Clifton leveled those bottle-green eyes straight at Gaspar. "Reacher called a guy out in a parking lot. A civilian. Can't remember the victim's name. He owned a local strip joint." His tone bordered on disgust. "He disabled the guy with a kick to the knee. Took him down. Guy was never the same again. A fellow officer filed a formal complaint. Reacher admitted what he'd done and we busted him back. We'd have saved everybody a lot of trouble if we'd shipped him to Leavenworth with the others."

I was visualizing the fight in my head. I saw Reacher cocking one giant foot and driving his heel into Alvin Barry's right kneecap with every ounce of force his two hundred thirty pounds could deliver, blasting right through him hard enough to shatter the patella and fold the man's leg backward. Alvin would have fallen forward. Reacher would have smiled. Maybe even thought to himself something like *he shoots, he scores.*

Alvin Barry must have felt like a Mack truck ran him down. A Broken bone, torn cartilage, ripped ligaments. I remembered Junior's anger and vows of revenge. I shuddered.

But Clifton's reaction confused me because he'd said *people* were unhappy with Reacher's abuse of Alvin, but I got the feeling that Clifton was ambivalent. "So, you think what Reacher did was okay, or not okay?"

He flashed the withering stare he'd used to quell armed combat troops at fifty paces. "Reacher was wearing his Class As at the time. Complete with name tag. Everyone standing around watching knew exactly who he was. An officer. In the U.S. Army. He disgraced us all."

The way he delivered this made it abundantly clear that what Reacher did would have been okay with General Matthew Clifton if only he'd done it while wearing jeans and a T-shirt, so nobody knew he was supposed to act like an officer and a gentleman. I shuddered again. Good to know.

"When did you see Reacher last?"

"When he was offered the opportunity to retire. Offered against my advice, by the way. He'd earned his way back. I'd have kept him on. I have no idea what he's doing now or where he's doing it or to whom. I couldn't help you find him if I wanted to. Which I don't. Pass that along to Cooper and Finlay for me. Tell them they're barking up the wrong tree and to stay out of my way." He grabbed his hat off the desk and strode toward the exit.

"One more thing, General." He stopped at the threshold and glanced back. "When was the last time you saw Joe Reacher?"

The question seemed to surprise and soften him some. His tone was slightly less hostile when he replied. "Couple of weeks before he died. We had dinner in DC. Damn shame about Joe. He was a hell of a man. Anything else?"

Clifton was about to walk out on us. I wanted to shake him up. I guessed Tony Clifton had some reason for sending me in this direction and Tony knew what my assignment was, but I didn't see any connection between the Reacher file and Matthew Clifton at all.

So I thought about the timing. I remembered how close Joe's ex-wife said the Reacher brothers were. How they were both officers in the Army back in 1990. Joe in Military Intelligence. Jack in Special Investigations. Summer right there with Jack.

Now, Joe was dead and Jack was missing.

Summer was the thread I needed to unravel.

From there, the Boss had expected me to dig into things and follow the trail to find out something Matthew Clifton might be hiding.

What was I supposed to uncover? And, once found, what was I supposed to do about it?

I still didn't know enough. But I knew Summer was involved in the old JAG case and I added two plus two and took a wild zag. To get his attention. Maybe shake something loose. Shake him up, if nothing else.

"Did Joe tell you about the affair with Eunice Summer?"

I meant the situation with Summer. But he interpreted the word differently.

He reared back a little as though startled to have the subject raised, then shrugged. "As far as I know, it wasn't a big thing," he said. "A couple of days in Paris at Uncle Sam's expense. Believe me, he's done much worse."

I blinked and shook my head to clear the cobwebs. What the hell was he talking about? Joe Reacher had a *love affair* with Eunice Summer? When did *that* happen? "I thought you said Joe was a hell of a man. Globetrotting with a lover at government expense doesn't seem like the behavior of a straight-up guy to me, General."

This time, he blinked. Then he smiled. "You're right. Not the sort of thing Joe Reacher would have done at all. My sergeant will see you out."

After he had left, Gaspar turned to me and said, "What a load of bullshit."

I nodded, but my head was still spinning. I'd been half a second too slow and now the opportunity was lost.

I'd made two mistakes. I'd phrased my question sloppily. I'd asked about the Summer affair when I'd simply meant the Summer situation.

But Clifton interpreted the word in the sexual sense *because he knew Summer had a love affair.*

My second mistake was to quickly assume Joe Reacher was Summer's lover because we'd been discussing Clifton's last meal with Joe. And because Jack hadn't been in the frame for a long, long time before I showed up in Clifton's office.

Which was a stupid leap and I should have known it.

But now I knew something I hadn't known before. Jack Reacher and Eunice Summer were lovers once. Which probably didn't matter to anyone at the time.

I now understood why the Boss had sent me to interview Summer. He knew she was in trouble, and figured Reacher, with his connections, might've known about it, too. He thought Reacher might show up to take care of the problem. But if

Reacher was coming, he was already too late to help Summer if that's what he meant to do.

I shook my head again as if I could rearrange my gray cells into a coherent picture. It didn't work.

What the hell was going on here? Was Reacher the cause or the effect of this situation? And why did the Boss and Finlay care?

CHAPTER TWENTY-TWO

AT THE FORT HERALD exit gate, Gaspar handed our visitor's pass to the sentry.

"Thanks." The sentry passed a flat manila envelope to Gaspar.

He looked at the envelope and asked, "Where'd this come from?"

"It was here when I came on duty, sir."

Gaspar nodded and passed the envelope to me. It was exactly like the previous envelope I'd received from the sentry at Fort Bird. Flat, manila, letter-sized. My name was printed on the front like before.

Gaspar reached into his pocket and handed me his knife. The sentry raised the gate and Gaspar rolled through.

I slit the bottom edge of the envelope with the knife and pushed the sides together to look inside. A written report. The title of which was *Eunice Summer Autopsy*.

Waiting for proper documenting of the envelope's contents was less important to me than reading the report. I grabbed a tissue and pulled the report out carefully without touching it.

Three pages. But the most important information was near the top. My breath drew sharply and painfully into my lungs.

Cause of Death: Gunshot.

"What is it?" Gaspar glanced toward me for an instant. Traffic was heavy and drivers seemed a little crazy around here. He kept both hands on the wheel and both eyes on the road.

I shook my head in reply, opened my personal phone and found the number I'd stored there. Then I pulled a burner cell phone out of my bag and dialed. It rang four times.

"Agent Otto." Lamont Finlay's rich Boston accent was unmistakable. "Can you join me at the Dallas Four Seasons? We have much to discuss."

"Affirmative," I replied and disconnected.

Calling was a necessary risk. The burner cell was not on the Boss's watch list yet and by the time he discovered the number, I'd have ditched it. But the rental Crown Vic was equipped with all manner of tracking and listening devices he could hack into. Not to mention the secure cell phones we carried in the vehicle, which might even be able to read our minds by this point for all I knew.

I read the rest of the autopsy report quickly.

When Gaspar merged onto the Interstate, moving smoothly with the flow of traffic, I said, "Take the spur into the city. We need to get some dinner before we fly back to New Haven."

He asked no further questions. He'd be no more anxious to have the Boss's nose in that report than I was. We'd discuss it soon enough.

The report's physical description haunted me. In life, Eunice Summer had been barely larger than me. She'd weighed 120 pounds, fully dressed. She was short and slender, but O'Connor said she'd carried herself like a catwalk model. Even in the autopsy photos, her skin was the color of finely burnished mahogany.

In death, well, there wasn't much left of her to weigh and measure after they finally extracted her body from the tortured metal. It was a minor miracle that he'd found evidence of the gunshot wound to her head, given the condition of her body, the medical examiner said. He must have done some kind of skull fragment reconstruction or computer modeling or something.

No bullet was recovered from the body or the wreckage or at the scene. Probably because no one had been looking for bullets. The crash had been more than enough to have killed her. Most times, the obvious cause is enough. There'd have been no reason for the crime scene techs to suspect another mechanism in play.

The shooter must have been counting on that because placing a bullet in her head under those conditions—small vehicle traveling fast, other vehicles around, icy roads, fog, wind, and rain? Not many assassins in the world could have done it.

There was a time when Jack Reacher possessed such skills. Safe to assume he still did.

Gaspar parked the Crown Vic and I gestured to leave our phones in the vehicle. The Boss would find us soon enough. We didn't need a beacon to guide him.

Not until we were walking from the parking lot toward the Four Seasons entrance did Gaspar ask, "What's going on here, Sunshine?"

I lowered my voice to blend in with ambient noises. "The envelope we just got didn't come from the Boss. Finlay sent it. He might have sent the first one, too."

Gaspar scowled. He trusted Finlay even less than he trusted

the Boss. I handed him the envelope. He scanned the autopsy report as we walked.

Summer's cause of death was first. When Gaspar saw it, his eyebrows shot up, but unlike me, he kept breathing even as he reached the next grabber. *Manner of death: Homicide.* His eyes moved quickly over the rest. When he finished, he folded the report lengthwise and tucked it into the breast pocket of his jacket.

I'd pulled the burner phone apart and dropped pieces of it into a series of trash barrels as we passed them.

We'd stepped five feet inside the lobby of the hotel when a dark-suited, well-proportioned man approached us. I'd seen hundreds of guys like him before. Unmistakably high-level government official security detail.

"Otto, Gaspar, this way, please." We followed him into a crowded elevator and then down a long corridor on the top floor to Suite 4. He opened the door with a key and moved aside.

Lamont Finlay, Ph.D., stood across the open room looking exactly as he'd looked the last time I saw him. Like a prosperous financial planner to the rich and famous.

Tall, straight, solid. Close-cropped hair slightly gray at the temples. Eyes the color of cognac. Clean-shaven. Well dressed. Everything polished to high gloss. Distinguished. Experienced. Intimidating as hell.

A black man, but his ethnicity was not African-American. The file said his grandparents had emigrated from Trinidad to New York before settling in Boston, where he'd been educated at Harvard. The Boston accent had faded, but I could still hear it.

Finlay had been selected by the highest-ranking civilian responsible for Homeland Security and Counterterrorism, placed one heartbeat away from the U.S. Commander-in-Chief. No watchdog kept tabs on him. He reported seldom and only through verbal briefing. No paper trail so much as named the missions he'd undertaken. Process, performance, results, also absent from the record.

Casualties, of course, never acknowledged. I'd heard rumors. Unconfirmed.

Everything I'd learned about Finlay marked him as dangerous. He deployed unique, unspecified skills in service to the country on unidentified missions. Like nuclear power, when properly harnessed he might be useful. But I'd found nothing restraining him. Not even his own word.

Was he friend or foe? Wiser to assume the worst was what Gaspar had declared the answer.

We entered Finlay's suite and our escort closed the door behind him, presumably remaining in the corridor to guard the entrance.

As Gaspar bee-lined for the room service pastries and coffee Finlay had ordered, Finlay's mouth lifted slightly at the corners. "Help yourself."

Gaspar ignored him.

"What's this about?" I asked. Finlay was at least as powerful as the Boss and could help me or hurt me at least as effectively. The last time I'd been in a similar hotel room with Finlay, I'd been nervous and intimidated, off my game. I'd vowed the next time I saw him would be different.

"You read the autopsy report. And saw the crash views. You know Colonel Summer was murdered. You must at least suspect that Cooper sent you to Fort Bird at that precise point in time because he knew the murder was planned. And he believed Reacher would be there. Maybe he believes Reacher killed her."

"We're not Western Union," Gaspar said, munching. His

patience for Finlay and for Finlay's jousting with Cooper had been exhausted long ago. "You know more about it than we do. Ask him yourself."

"I gave you the facts, questions, Gaspar." Finlay remained unruffled, as always. Which was one of the things that made Gaspar suspicious of him. Finlay had something to hide, for sure. But then, who didn't?

"We didn't see Reacher," I said before they squared off and started beaking each other like fighting cocks. "If that's what you wanted to know, you could have asked me on the phone. Saved us a trip."

"You didn't see him, but that doesn't mean he wasn't there," Finlay replied. "Reacher could have killed Summer. Maybe Cooper thinks he did."

"I don't know what the Boss thinks and neither do you," I said, as done with the Cooper/Finlay show as Gaspar was. "What's going on here?"

"We're not sure." Finlay opened his palm toward a seating area. I moved to one of the chairs and Finlay sat across from me. Gaspar remained bent over the pastry tray. "The Inspector General has been investigating General Matthew Clifton for three years. We believe he's involved in high-level corruption surrounding weapons-building for The Big War."

"But they can't prove it," Gaspar said, derision as thick as the cream and sugar in his coffee.

"Not yet."

"Is Thomas O'Connor involved?" I asked.

"We're not sure. But you know his wife was Reacher's sister-in-law?"

"Briefly. A long time ago. She doesn't even know Joe Reacher is dead, she claims."

Finlay remained silent, possibly waiting for us to formulate some conclusions on our own, or deciding what to reveal and what to withhold. Or maybe something else altogether. My mind-reading skills failed me yet again.

"How is Reacher involved in all of this?" I asked, a little irked at this point.

Gaspar laughed out loud. "Didn't you hear the man? He's not sure."

Finlay smiled benignly at him. "You'd be dead now if it wasn't for me," he pointed out, not unreasonably. "Several times, in fact. And yet, such disrespect."

Gaspar shrugged, but he didn't argue.

"The Boss says you're the dangerous one," I said to Finlay. "Obviously, there's no love lost between you." I squared my shoulders and sat up as tall as a 4'11" woman can sit. "And we work for him. So why are we here?"

"You're building this Reacher file. Or so you think." Finlay rubbed a palm along one side of his mahogany face, which was almost the same color as Summers' had been. A luminous shade of coppery brown. "Let me help you out. What do you know about Eunice Summer?"

"Not much," Gaspar snapped. I glared at him, but he glared right back. I'd warned him about baiting Finlay, but he wouldn't listen.

Finlay's tone was even and, as always, unperturbed. "She and Reacher solved a corruption scandal that could have brought the weight of the entire world down on the Army's top brass back in 1990. Not just internal squabbling. Internecine warfare, complete with assassinations and considerable collateral damage. Reacher got himself into some unrelated trouble and bailed out. She ran with the prosecution."

"Yeah, we know all of that," Gaspar said, fudging the truth, probably to appear unimpressed. He claimed a chair and slouched.

Finlay ignored him. "Since 1990, Summer has made it her business to investigate corruption complaints. If corruption is alleged, she chases it down until she's satisfied. Then she pushes for courts-martial and makes sure the guilty ones are locked up forever."

"That's gotta make her popular at the Officer's Club," Gaspar said, munching and sipping. "Increases the suspect pool."

"Actually, she built solid cases and then she took them up the chain of command and then the Army handled them—out of the spotlight, which the top brass did appreciate, believe me. They don't like reading about their dirty laundry in the *New York Times* and the *Washington Post* and having it beamed across the world to our enemies." He crossed his long legs and leaned back, open and easygoing. "But, sure, the ones who were prosecuted weren't happy. Neither were their friends. She made enemies. Powerful ones."

I leaned forward. "So she was working on a corruption case when she died. Same as most days. You're suggesting someone killed her for that?" What he said rang true. There must have been a connection, but it was hard to see what that relationship might be. "And why would Reacher care about corruption in the Army now? He's been out of that life for fifteen years."

"The important thing for you to know is that Cooper believes Reacher cares. Probably because of Summer. Reacher has a tendency to be protective of his friends and deadly to his enemies." Finlay looped one leg over the other and kicked back. I've seen men discussing weekend sports get a lot more agitated than Finlay discussing murder and mayhem. Might have been an act, but my gut said he was exactly as calm as he appeared.

Gaspar said, "You sound like you've got firsthand knowledge. What are you to Reacher? Friend or enemy?"

Finlay ignored him. To me, he said, "Cooper thought you'd find Reacher. That's why he sent you to Fort Bird. So you could sniff Reacher out."

Yeah, tell me something I don't know. The tension in my neck and shoulders made it hard to move my head. "And this interests you because?"

Gaspar had refilled his coffee. "Because Finlay doesn't want Cooper to find Reacher before he does. Plain as the nose on his face."

I shook my head. "That's not quite right, is it, Finlay? You'd rather Reacher wasn't found at all, I'm guessing."

Finlay revealed his teeth, but the expression wasn't a smile. Not even remotely. "My reasons are my own. All you need to know is that Cooper's using you. And it could get you killed."

"Yeah, well, that's old news, too," Gaspar assured him.

"You're worried, aren't you?" I stood and faced Finlay. "If Cooper wants us to flush Reacher out, which we all suspect is exactly what he wants, then you want the same thing. Only you want to get to Reacher first."

"Not quite." Finlay shook his head slightly. "I'd be fine with Reacher staying off the grid for the rest of his life. But I don't want Cooper to find him."

"Why do you care?" Gaspar asked.

"The sniper who killed Summer had to be military trained. Probably Army or Marines. Reacher has both types of training. Garden variety snipers couldn't have done it. The circumstances of that shoot were not impossible, but well beyond merely difficult. He pulled it off." He paused and bent his head in a brief, single nod. "Be afraid, Otto. If you won't trust me to help you, fear is the only thing that might keep you alive."

He'd confirmed one thing for sure. Any of the more than a million active and inactive Army co-workers could have had reasons to want Eunice Summer dead. A twenty-five-year career chasing Army crimes would have put a target on her back many times over. Narrowing the suspect pool would be a challenge for an entire task force. Gaspar and I would never manage it if we used conventional techniques.

Finlay stood and shot the stiff cuffs of his white shirt. Gleaming gold cufflinks caught the light. He smoothed his tie over his plank-flat stomach and buttoned his jacket.

"This is a two-bedroom suite," he said. "It's yours for the night. Order dinner. Get some sleep. Think about what I've said."

After he had left, Gaspar picked up the room service menu. He grinned. "This is a lot nicer than ordering stale sandwiches from the truck stop delivered to the New Haven Grand Lodge by an exotic dancer."

I swiped a room key off the table. "Let's go get your pajamas."

On the way back from the car, I used my personal cell phone to dial Sheriff Randy Taylor and arranged to meet him at the morgue tomorrow. I wanted to see Summer's body for myself and I didn't care who knew I was coming.

CHAPTER TWENTY-THREE

THE SUITE AT THE Four Seasons was more than a few classes up from the New Haven Grand Lodge, for sure. Each bedroom was larger than my apartment and furnished with a king bed and a desk. The only downside was the near certainty that the Boss could see and hear everything that went on inside.

Unless of course Finlay had disabled the security and probably his own while he was here. He might have returned all systems to normal by now.

Either way, the safe assumption was that anything we said or did here would be like simultaneously broadcasting on television, radio, and the Internet.

But then, both Finlay and Cooper already knew more than we did about whatever was going on here, so unless we came up with something remarkable, in theory, there was nothing to worry about.

Neither of us was dressed for the Four Seasons' dining room, so we ordered room service off the menu. While we waited for delivery, I unpacked and washed off the road grime in a shower large enough for a party. Afterward, I felt almost human again.

A doorbell chimed. Gaspar was talking on the phone in his

room, probably to Marie, so I answered it. Room service delivered and set up and left and never asked me to sign anything. Finlay's doing, I imagined. The paperwork would never show we were here.

While I waited for Gaspar, I set up my laptop and connected to the secure satellite. Nothing pending from the Boss. Which might be okay if he hadn't seen the Summer autopsy report yet. If he had seen the report, then failing to send it to us was not okay at all.

I wrote up my notes for the results of our assignment so far and uploaded them to my secure personal server along with a copy of the autopsy report. Paying my insurance premium, I call it. Just in case something goes wrong down the line. My gut said that day was coming. I could feel it the way an arthritic feels a coming storm.

Gaspar was still on the phone and my stomach was growling. To distract myself and simply for practice, I checked the suite for electronic eavesdropping equipment. Which was when I noticed another flat manila envelope. This one was resting on the chair Finlay had occupied earlier. Had he left it there?

It had my name on the front in the now familiar printing. Still flat, but a bit heftier than the last one. I found a butter knife to slit the bottom seal open.

Inside were several photographs. I turned the envelope upside down and poured eight eight-by-ten photos onto my bed. Using a tissue, I arranged them in what seemed like chronological order.

I was still studying them when Gaspar finished his call and yelled from the other room, "Aren't you hungry?"

When I didn't answer, he came through the open doorway. "What do you have there?"

"I'm not sure."

Gaspar joined me at the side of the bed and we both stared down at the photos.

Six of the photos were stills from a closed-circuit video system. The poor quality of the images suggested older equipment. There was no date or time stamp. The seventh photo was an outdoor shot of a residential neighborhood. The eighth was a crime scene.

Each of the first six images was a man and a woman. The man was huge. The woman was petite.

In the first photo, the scene was a hotel lobby. The man and woman faced the registration desk. Both were dressed in BDUs. The clerk was totally obscured by the man's oversized body, which probably meant the clerk was female. A sign behind and above the desk clerk's head said "Georges V."

The second photo was the man and woman coming out of the elevator. She must have been talking because his head was bent as if to hear her. His face was obscured. Hers was clear enough to recognize. Eunice Summer. I imagined the colors, copper behind the deep mahogany of her skin, coal-black eyes, and delicate jaw. She was beautiful and young. Maybe about twenty-five years old.

The third photo was the pair walking into the hotel through the front entrance. A man with a top hat held the door open. Each carried a Samaritaine shopping bag, presumably filled with the BDUs because now they wore civilian clothes. Black shoes, black pencil skirt, gray and white sweater, and a gray wool jacket for her. He'd donned jeans, a light blue sweatshirt, and a black bomber jacket. He was still wearing his Army boots, presumably because he couldn't find shoes large enough. Both wore jaunty berets. Again, his head was tilted down as if to hear her words and his face was obscured.

I studied the fourth photo for a while. They were exiting the elevator again. They wore smiles and the civilian clothes, minus the berets. This time, both faces were identifiable. Summer's companion was Jack Reacher. No question. Travel documents could confirm, if we needed confirmation.

Aside from his formal Army headshot and some grainy outdoor video, this was the first time I'd seen a full frontal image. He was handsome in a rugged, weathered way. Fair hair was cut short in the Army style. Blue eyes with a few squint lines at the corners like he'd spent a lot of time outdoors in the sunshine.

He carried himself squared away, like the model for a child's action figure doll. Tall, broad-shouldered, well-muscled. Huge hands and feet. Overall, he looked young and happy and world-weary, all at the same time.

The fifth photo was the pair returning to the hotel again. The man with the top hat held the door. Reacher and Summer held hands. Hers was invisible inside his giant paw.

The sixth photo was the one paparazzi would call the money shot. It was edited from video captured by a corridor camera.

Reacher was standing just inside the open door to her room, still wearing the jeans and a blue sweatshirt. Barefoot. Summer was dressed in her civilian clothes, too. They were kissing. The kind of kissing that usually led to a lot more intimate contact. In an old-fashioned movie, this would be the part where he'd kick the door closed, leaving us to imagine the rest. Not that much imagination was required.

So Reacher and Summer were lovers. Together in Paris. Doing the quick math in my head, it had to have been around the same time Josephine Reacher died.

The last two photos were completely different. Different

time, different place, different camera. Different subjects, too. Jarringly so.

The seventh photo was of a dead man seated on a kitchen floor, legs straight out, arms to his sides, hands resting on the floor, with a gunshot wound through the center of his forehead. Gray hair parted and combed to the side and a little too long around his ears. Steel-rimmed eyeglasses magnified his eyes, which were wide open as if he'd been well and truly shocked to see the bullet coming. Unlike the others, this photo had a date and military time stamp. 13-1-90. 1932.

The eighth and last photo was the backyard of a house on a residential street after dark. A single streetlight in the alley provided weak yellow illumination. The yard was messy. An old barbecue grill had been tossed on the ground in the middle of what might once have been a lawn. A big man wearing woodland-patterned BDUs and boots was in the process of walking out the back door when the photo was taken. The date and time stamp was 13-1-90. 1934.

"Where did these come from?" Gaspar asked after a while.

"I found another envelope in Finlay's chair, but I didn't see it until after the room service guy left." My stomach growled loud enough to be heard all the way to Paris. I grabbed my phone and took pictures of the photos and sent them to my personal server.

"Let's eat." Gaspar walked toward the sitting room. "We can talk at the same time. The Boss and Finlay already know all of this, so if you missed any bugs during your search of the rooms earlier, they wouldn't hear anything new."

Our food had been sent up inside one of those carts that keeps everything warm until you're ready and then it opens into a table. Gaspar pulled the plates out and I poured the water. I handed him the wine bottle and the corkscrew.

Once we were sorted, I said, "So Reacher and Summer-the-sanctimonious-bulldog had an affair, maybe on Uncle Sam's dime, and General Clifton and Joe probably knew about it. Who else knew?"

Gaspar chewed his steak like a man just released from indenture. "Maybe no one. At least, not back then. Because Reacher was Summer's CO, too. The Army still takes a dim view of that kind of fraternizing."

"Looks like they were already in all kinds of deep shit, though. I mean, what kind of Army grunt can afford to stay at the Georges V? That's the place Princess Diana stayed. Royalty and business tycoons and wealthy oil sheiks sleep there. Hell, two nights in that place and you'd have to mortgage all five of your kids to pay the bill, Chico."

Gaspar grinned. "A little bit like either of us trying to pay for this suite, eh?"

"It explains why the Boss thought Reacher might show up at Fort Bird, though. I mean, Summer was supposed to be there to tell me all about it, remember?"

"It was a one-night stand, Suzy Wong. Not *Casablanca*. He wouldn't care if we found out about the whole thing after all this time." Gaspar cut off another chunk of the steak and stuck it in his mouth. "Didn't she tell you she hadn't seen Reacher in twenty years? Kind of suggests he never saw her again after he left Fort Bird, anyway."

"Yeah, well, by all accounts they weren't sleeping together in the most expensive hotel in Paris, either." I'd been pushing my food around on the plate, but that wasn't helping my grouchy stomach. So I ate. The veal piccata was excellent, if a little cold.

"Drink some more wine." He grinned and refilled my glass. What he meant was that I should chill out. These photos were decades old. Summer was dead and Reacher was, well, not around. So far. How could their affair and who funded it possibly matter now?

Which was exactly the problem. The affair shouldn't have mattered. But somehow, it did. Mattered enough that Finlay left that envelope with the photos in it. Or the Boss sent them up with the room service guy. Or someone else made sure we found them. Either way, the clear message was that the old affair was important.

I played with the veal and capers and thought about why that might be.

The only motive that made sense was blackmail. Summer had spent her career ferreting out corruption. Yet she'd been AWOL at the Army's expense in Paris while sleeping with her commanding officer. How much more against the rules could her behavior have possibly been?

If this evidence of criminal and ethical misbehavior was made public now, she'd have been reprimanded, at the very least. She might even have been busted back, the way Reacher had been. Conduct unbecoming and all of that. Given the Army's constant force reductions, she might have been encouraged to retire, too. Maybe she'd have paid to keep the truth under wraps. The blackmailer might have tried Reacher, too, assuming he could find Reacher. But Reacher had nothing to lose and Summer had everything to lose. She was the logical target.

The only problem with the blackmail theory was that it's impossible to blackmail a dead woman.

Which meant sending us the photos now, when Summer was already dead, had to be motivated by something else entirely.

CHAPTER TWENTY-FOUR

WE TOOK A NONSTOP from Dallas to Raleigh the next morning and collected another Crown Vic at the airport that Gaspar had somehow acquired. With Gaspar behind the wheel, we traveled the Interstate south this time. The same route Summer would have taken on the day she died. Gaspar drove the speed limit, which gave me a chance to observe the terrain, had there been anything to see.

We rode most of the distance with our own thoughts and no conversation, which was fine with me. I've never understood why two people alone in a car or a room necessarily had to talk to each other.

North of the exit for New Haven, *The Lucky Bar's* neon signs flashed blindingly. Which probably meant they were once again open for business.

Gaspar said, "Do we have time to look around at the truck stop?"

"After. I want to have plenty of time for mile marker #224."

The Crown Vic was cruising at the posted speed limit of seventy miles an hour when we passed the truck stop. We had been gradually gaining elevation and ten miles further along, we began our descent. The road wasn't particularly dangerous. It wound through picturesque mountainous woodland from well before the truck stop all the way past Fort Bird.

"Around that blind curve is the spot. Right lane."

At mile marker #224, the pavement curved a wide left bank and disappeared around the mountain.

Gaspar slowed well below the minimum speed and turned on his flashers as if he was having engine problems. The incline had been gradual, but the descent was steeper. Warning signs were posted before the curve and more lined the guardrail along the big bend.

The blind curve was perfectly safe at the posted speed limit, which was reduced to fifty miles an hour. At eighty miles an hour, it would be maybe half as safe.

I wasn't driving this time, which meant I could take my eyes off the road to scan the area thoroughly.

The right side guardrail was damaged. Whether from Summer's crash or an earlier one was impossible to say.

After the shoulder on the far right southbound lane, the mountain fell away. Nothing but treetops filled the void. An involuntary shudder ran through me when I peered over the guardrail down the steep incline on the right.

"So the first rig was either slowed or stopped ahead and Summer had no time to avoid the crash," Gaspar said.

"That's what the report says, and how it probably unfolded based on the photo as well as the newscast videos we've seen."

"Why did the tanker in front of Summer stop along here? Anybody would recognize the danger. Semi drivers are pros. They wouldn't create a potential safety disaster like that."

"He says he had already slowed due to the weather

conditions. When he came around the blind curve, there were two deer crossing the road and he downshifted and braked to slow further. He said he was moving when she hit him, but not fast enough to avoid the collision."

"Could have happened that way. Any reason to believe otherwise?"

"Not that I've heard. Finlay's photo was snapped pretty quickly and shows no deer on the roadway. But deer are fast and there's no traffic cam video, either. So the story hasn't been confirmed or disproved."

"What happened to the traffic cams?"

Good question. I craned my neck to peer at the top of the utility poles where the traffic cams were perched, as they should have been. "Malfunction, I guess."

Gaspar snorted. "All of them? Only in this one spot? Unlikely. Another question for the Boss."

There was no place to pull off the road or move into the median to stop for a closer look at the scene, so Gaspar turned off the flashers and increased speed on the other side of the curve.

Twelve miles farther down the road was the exit for Fort Bird. Gaspar exited the highway, turned left at the end of the ramp, and reentered the highway on the other side.

When we approached the accident scene headed north, we were on the inside traffic lanes, hugging the jagged wall of mountain rock that abutted the far right northbound lane.

The blind curve ahead seemed like driving into empty air from this direction as if we were continuing based on nothing but faith in American highway engineering.

The only additional safety features of the northbound side were the solid mountain on the right and the climbing elevation that slowed traffic.

When we were well past mile marker #224, I unbuckled my seatbelt and crabbed into the back seat to retrieve the Boss's padded envelope. When I re-settled into the front passenger seat, I ripped open the envelope and powered up the secure cell phone.

"Need a charger?" Gaspar asked.

I gave him my best imitation of a teenagers' total exasperation with the stupidity of parents. "Oh, please. Seriously? This phone came from the Boss and you think it could possibly be less than ready?"

He grinned. "Right. What was I thinking?"

We drove back to the New Haven exit, left the highway, and did the circuit again. By that time, I'd found the video camera on the secure cell phone and flipped it to record from a mile north of the scene.

I panned the area, documenting everything as well as possible. When we'd traveled a mile past the point of impact, I stopped recording and sent the video to my secure server via satellite. I repeated the process on the way back.

We didn't speak because we wanted no audio on the recording.

After the second recording was secure, Gaspar said, "Send a text. Tell him the video is on the way and send it to him."

I'd already started the process. I tossed him a scathing glance. "You think you're the only one in this vehicle who wants to save our skin, Che?"

"Very often, Helga, that's precisely what I think." He only called me Helga when what he meant was that I was as stubborn as any German on the planet. *Damn straight.*

We continued the rest of the way to the New Haven exit in silence. Instead of turning right toward *The Lucky Bar* and the Grand Lodge, the GPS directed Gaspar to turn left.

We had traveled five miles before we reached the New Haven Hospital, where Sheriff Taylor had said the local pathologist doubled as the local medical examiner.

Taylor's empty cruiser was parked near the side entrance. Gaspar parked the Crown Vic next to Taylor's and we hustled out. I placed the flat of my palm on the hood of Taylor's cruiser as we passed. He must have arrived only a few minutes before we did because the hood of the cruiser was still warm.

We found him inside the modern autopsy room decorated with easy-to-clean shiny surfaces, talking with a man wearing green hospital scrubs.

"Sheriff Taylor, this is my partner, Agent Carlos Gaspar," I said as we walked up to the two men standing over a steel shelf that had been pulled out from a refrigerator in the wall.

Taylor nodded to Gaspar and introduced the pathologist, Dr. Smith. The unrecognizably mangled body on the steel shelf had once been Eunice Summer, but the only way I could confirm that was by reading the toe tag. Somehow, her body hadn't seemed quite so mangled in the photographs I'd already seen.

"You've read the autopsy report?" Dr. Smith asked. "Not much more to add, I'm afraid. Cause of death was definitely the gunshot wound to her head though she'd have died on impact with that tanker if she hadn't been dead already."

The matter-of-fact delivery style was one I'd encountered from medical examiners before. A coping mechanism or something. No human being charged with caring for the sick could possibly be so lacking in sensitivity otherwise.

"How can you be sure about the gunshot?" Gaspar asked. "There's not much evidence here to work with."

"Dumb luck, actually." Dr. Smith pointed to a sharp skull fragment over Summer's right ear. The bony fragment was less than an inch wide and maybe half again as long. "See this here? It's a fragment. But it's the size and shape a bullet normally makes when it hits this location on the human skull. Nothing else can cause that precise type of hole in that particular bone."

"If you say so," I replied. Because the whole body was such a mess that the thing he said was a bullet hole looked like another shard to me.

"I do say so. And I'll say it under oath on the witness stand if you find the man who shot her, too. It's murder, pure and simple." Dr. Smith's cold delivery had heated up. Turned out he wasn't as indifferent to murder as he was to death, I guess.

"Anybody find the bullet for comparison?" I asked Taylor.

He shook his head. "It may be out there somewhere, but we'd have to close the Interstate for a month to find it. Even then, we'd have to get damn lucky."

Dr. Smith sighed. "If she hadn't been dead already, she might have avoided that collision. There's two lanes at that point and she was a good driver. She might have gone around. She would have slowed down, at the very least. It's possible she could have survived."

"What about the second truck, though?" Gaspar asked. "He'd have still hit her car from the rear. She wasn't likely to have survived the double impact, was she?"

Dr. Smith deflated. "Probably not. But she might have, is the point."

We stood looking at Summer for a bit longer, but the realities didn't change.

I asked, "What about the other bodies? The ones from *The Lucky Bar*?"

"Much more obvious gunshot wounds and cause of death for all of those. I'm still sorting through which guns and which bullets were the fatal ones, but nothing mysterious about any of them."

Taylor said, "Thanks, Doc. I think we're done here, aren't we, Otto?"

"Almost. Dr. Smith, do you have any personal effects from any of these victims?"

"Over here, I think." He led the group to a steel autopsy table where he'd laid out the personal effects for each of the bodies prior to bagging and marking them as evidence.

On the steel slab were the accumulated possessions of the four soldiers and the dancer and her ex-boyfriend or ex-husband or whatever kind of ex he was.

The soldiers carried wallets and keys and a bit of pocket change. They wore belts and watches. Precious little and nothing worth killing them for that I could see.

The dancer was naked at the time she was killed. Her possessions were four pierced earrings and a diamond-like stud from her naval piercing.

The man who shot them all had no more in his pockets than the others. But around his neck, he'd worn a gold chain. I'd seen the glinting in the green strobe lights the night he died. The chain wasn't among the items in his meager pile of belongings.

I looked at Dr. Smith. "Where's his neck chain?"

Taylor replied for him. "It's in another evidence bag. Because of the contents."

"Contents?" Gaspar said. "Of a neck chain?"

"Not the chain. The pendant. Dr. Smith, can you get that for us, too?"

Dr. Smith walked to another cabinet, unlocked it with a key from his key ring, and returned with a clear plastic evidence bag that had been marked with his initials and sealed. He handed it to me first.

Inside the bag was a heavy serpentine gold chain with a lobster claw clasp. Maybe about eighteen inches long. The kind men wore back in the 1990s.

Dangling from the chain was a crystal vial that looked like a large capsule. It seemed like it would twist apart in the middle to allow the removal of the object inside. Which looked exactly like a shiny gold bullet. A standard nine-millimeter Parabellum, to be exact. Full metal jacket.

I'd seen similar mementos before. For some reason, men mostly seemed to want to hold on to bullets similar to the ones that hit them. Rites of passage or something, I guess. Probably made for some good cocktail party chatter in the right crowds.

I held the evidence bag up to the light for a better view of the bullet. It seemed to have some sort of etching on it. I couldn't quite make it out inside all the layers of the bag. "Do you have a magnifying glass?"

A look passed between Sheriff Taylor and Dr. Smith that I made no effort to decipher. They'd both seen the neck chain and the bullet. Gaspar and I were playing catch-up.

Dr. Smith pulled a round disk mounted on a swing arm from one side of the steel table. He turned on the light that encircled the disk like a bathroom makeup mirror. I held the bag and the crystal capsule under the lighted magnifier and peered at the etching.

Under magnification, it was easy to read the single word scratched onto the bullet.

Reacher.

CHAPTER TWENTY-FIVE

I HANDED THE EVIDENCE bag to Gaspar and stepped aside to allow him access to the magnifying glass. He examined everything in the same way I had. When he finished, he handed the evidence bag back to Dr. Smith.

"Do we know anything about this guy yet?" I asked Sheriff Taylor.

"His name is Jeffrey Mayne. We ran him through the usual databases, but we found nothing that explains the bullet. He was a veteran. Delta Force. Stationed at Fort Bird back in 1988-90 time frame. Which probably means he knew his way around New Haven and was proficient with weaponry of all sorts."

"Was he a trained sniper?"

"Maybe," Taylor said. "We've contacted Major Clifton for help and requested Mayne's records from the Army, but they're a little slow in producing them."

No shock there. "What about since the Army? Any intel on anything helpful?"

"Not much. He lived in Nashville, Tennessee. Worked for a defense contractor like a lot of these ex-military guys do."

The churning that had started in my stomach upon the discovery of Reacher's name on the bullet that Mayne wore around his neck was now turned up to a constant level of thrashing that was actually painful. I reached into my pocket for an antacid and placed it on my tongue.

"We called his office and spoke with his boss," Taylor said. "A guy named Thomas O'Connor. He's on his way here now. Probably arrive in a couple of hours, he said."

Mayne worked for O'Connor. That bit of news pushed my stomach to the two-antacid level.

"What about the bullet? Any idea what that's all about? Doesn't seem like it's ever been fired."

Taylor looked at Dr. Smith, who cleared his throat and said, "Right. Looks like it was lodged at one time in his nasal passages."

"I'm sorry?"

He gave a small shrug. "Appears to have been shoved up there pretty hard and then stayed there a while, because the scar tissue was an unmistakable match. He probably had serious breathing problems after that."

Dr. Smith pushed a couple of buttons and displayed an image on a small screen. This one was an autopsy photo showing Mayne's deformed nasal passages. He pointed out the scar tissue that, frankly, I'd never have found on my own. But once he showed it to us, the crater where that bullet had lodged was obvious.

"He'd have been a mouth-breather for a long time after that," Dr. Smith said. "Maybe forever."

Gaspar nodded.

We snapped a few photos of the bullet and the autopsy photo. When we'd seen everything, Taylor walked out with us.

"I'd like to show you something back at my station if you've got the time."

"What is it?" I stretched my neck and shoulders, working at the tension there. What I needed was a swim or a massage or even a few more hours sleep in a decent bed. Unfortunately, the Four Seasons and the Georges V were way out of my price range.

"That's what I want you to tell me. I'd rather not prejudice your first take on it."

"Lead the way," Gaspar said.

CHAPTER TWENTY-SIX

WE FOLLOWED SHERIFF TAYLOR to his station, which was a one-story, modern brick construction law enforcement building. The words New Haven Area Law Enforcement Center were prominently displayed on the side facing the main road.

The tax base in New Haven must have been healthier than I'd assumed. The building and everything in it would have been the envy of any municipality in America with fewer than a million residents.

Taylor led us to a conference room equipped with television screens on the walls. He used a remote to pull the four still images onto four of the screens so we could see them simultaneously.

The four were shot from a drone in and around Summer's murder scene. The big rigs, the crumpled red sports car, mile marker #224. No deer. All of it familiar by now because I'd seen it many times.

Taylor replaced these four images with four more. The second batch was sequential. Same scene, but photos were shot as if the drone was panning from behind the rear bumper of the second truck to beyond the front bumper of the first truck.

"Here is where Summer hit the tanker." Taylor used a laser to point out the relevant bits as he talked. "Our calculations say she was shot about here, fifty-three feet from the crash." He pointed to a stretch of the sloping highway just into the curve. "She had her wheels turned toward the curve or she'd have run off the mountain instead."

Gaspar said, "And if her vehicle had to travel a greater distance after she died, she'd have gone either off the side as she left the curve or she'd have run into oncoming traffic."

"Or she'd have run into the rock wall if there was no traffic," I added, moving my head from side-to-side for accurate views. "Which means that the sniper's window of opportunity was narrow and his aim was damn good."

Taylor loaded the next batch of photos, which were aerial shots of the crash scene from the valley side of the highway.

From that angle, I might have seen glimpses of Summer's body inside the wreckage. A couple of hours with an enlarged set of photos and establishing shots to compare the clothing on the woman in the vehicle to Summer's wardrobe would have confirmed my guesses, perhaps.

"We sent everything up to the FBI in DC. We should have confirmation and a reconstruction video soon." Taylor loaded the next set of photos and pointed with his laser to a spot of rocky land about 1500 yards away from the crash. "Once they crunch the numbers, we'll know more. But for now, we think the sniper was set up here."

The calculations might have taken hours back in the old days. But now, we had computer models that could handle the math swiftly once accurate data points for the conditions were acquired. Distance from the target, speed of the bullet, and speed of the target, bullet fall, and other variables could be determined in a flash.

The day Summer died presented just about the worst possible conditions for a long range sniper, but the closer he was to the target, the less things like heavy air would matter. The problem was, unless he had shimmied up a very tall tree, he wasn't close to the target. Almost a mile from it, if the computer's calculations were correct. Which proved he was a skilled marksman. More skilled than me.

The fact was, though, computers could only do what computers do and come up with the most likely scenario. A well-informed guess of the sniper's location, the type of gun and ammo he used, maybe even his probable height and weight.

And of course, he'd be long gone from that location now. Unless he'd left forensic evidence or the computer models could pinpoint identifying irregularities of some kind, none of this mattered. The exercise was intellectually interesting, but that was all.

The other thing was that if he'd shot from that location with an L115A3 rifle—as I suspected but so far could not confirm, so hadn't mentioned it—he'd have hit Summer harder than a 44 magnum inside her car. Which meant there wouldn't have been even a fragment of her skull left to reveal evidence of the kill, let alone a possible bullet hole fragment.

So he had to have been even farther away and an even better sniper than Taylor gave him credit for. Using Gaspar's observation about government record keeping and applying the tedious process of elimination, he could probably be identified. But it would take a while.

Taylor left the photos of the sniper's location on the screens and turned to me. "Agent Otto, I checked your credentials.

Gaspar, I checked yours, too. All three of us have had sniper training and we're all good with a rifle, but Otto's the best marksman in this room. What do you think about all of this?"

"We know Colonel Summer was murdered now," I said. "What we need to know is why there, why then, and why she was targeted."

He cocked his head as if my answer wasn't what he'd expected and he wanted to understand me.

"Look, the computers will figure out how this was done. You'll get as close to exact specs as possible and that will help you convict the sniper once he's found."

"Exactly," Taylor said.

"But there's more going on here, Sheriff."

"Meaning what?"

"This is about as premeditated a murder as you could possibly have. Nothing about this kill was dumb luck." I laid out my thinking to be sure he followed the logic. "First, he needed a precise plan. It's a tough shot. The terrain is a challenge. He'd have practiced. He wanted to get it right."

Taylor was nodding.

"Executing the plan that *particular* day and time must have been important, too. The shot was already going to be difficult under the best of circumstances. He had to hike in from somewhere, carrying his gear, and then hike out again."

He kept nodding.

"But that day, in addition to everything else he had to cope with, the weather was horrid. Worst possible conditions for a shot like that. Which increased his chance of failure exponentially."

"Uh, huh," he said.

"He could have chosen a different time, a different place. He could have shot her the day before or the day after. He could have set up closer to DC where the highway is flatter."

"And for the shot itself," Gaspar said, "a moment before or after and the sniper would have missed his chance."

"Which means he knew she was coming and he knew when she'd be passing that exact location," Taylor replied slowly, mulling things over.

I paced the room and waited for one of them to identify the really scary things. Because it sounded a lot more complicated than it actually was.

Taylor finally asked, "How many are involved? Three—the two truck drivers and the shooter?"

I heard the hope in his voice. To him, three was a manageable number. Small-time. Three made the killing feel more like a personal grudge. With three, he could find means, motive, and opportunity. Especially since he already knew who two of them were. He could squeeze the two truck drivers and maybe learn the identity of the sniper. Three meant he could solve the case and bring the killers to justice and restore order to his town.

Which was why I didn't say that three was nothing more than a good start.

CHAPTER TWENTY-SEVEN

IT WAS SUNDAY AND we were in the middle of the Bible belt, but *The Lucky Bar* had reopened for business. The flashing neon signs were unmistakable for both north and southbound traffic. Colonel Summer must have known precisely where she was whenever she drove past it over the years. No way could she have missed those lights, any more than she could have been disoriented or failed to realize that blind curve at mile marker #224.

Gaspar pulled into the truck stop to refuel and look around. It was getting late and we would stay at the New Haven Grand Lodge tonight.

"I thought you said Alvin Barry was hospitalized and his son, Junior, was arrested? Who's running the bar?"

I shrugged. It had been a long day. The last thing I'd hoped for was another trip to *The Lucky Bar*. But I knew that's exactly where I was headed.

Gaspar finished with the gas and we rolled over to *The Lucky Bar's* parking lot. There were fewer vehicles in the lot than there were two days ago, but it was still three-quarters full. Gaspar parked and we exited the vehicle. The bar's door was wide open and the wall of noise was palpable like before.

As we walked toward the entrance, Gaspar's limp grew less pronounced with each step, as always, yet he still pulled a Tylenol out of his pocket and swallowed it when he thought I wasn't looking. I was worried about his liver, but I said nothing. I was his partner, not his mother.

Once again, the stench of tobacco smoke and beer assaulted us more than ten yards away.

At the front door, we stopped briefly before stepping inside. Behind the bar was a younger, slightly smaller version of Junior Barry. Same stocky build, same tight black T-shirt, tattoos in all the same places.

Standing next to him was a woman I recognized. I nudged Gaspar with my elbow and nodded toward her. "Sergeant Major Madeline Jones, retired."

He nodded.

The pounding, pulsing country music and the garish pink, blue, and green floodlights supplied the necessary accompaniment for the exotic dancer on the stage. Tonight, the tables were upright and the chairs were full. Again, patrons seemed to be about ninety-eight percent male, mostly civilians, and a few enlisted men from Fort Bird looking uncomfortable in civilian clothes with unmistakable haircuts.

Everything about the place seemed to be business as usual like the shooting never happened.

Jones recognized me. She waited until we found an empty table near the back of the crowded floor where the din was slightly quieter and conversation almost possible. She brought over three domestic beers in brown long-necked bottles and joined us. She raised her bottle in a toast. "Thank you for your help with Alvin and Junior the other night," she shouted over the music.

"I wish I could have done more," I shouted back. I introduced Gaspar and she nodded and raised her bottle in his direction.

Gaspar took a sip to be friendly, but he normally didn't drink. I assumed he was worried about navigating on his bad leg while under the influence. Or maybe he was worried about his liver because all of the Tylenol he ate, too.

"You just helping out for tonight?"

"Alvin's my brother. I watch the place a couple of nights a week so he can get a break. We never had a shooting before, but things can get out of hand pretty quickly. That's a cousin behind the counter now. Everybody will be taking turns until Alvin is back on his feet and Junior is sorted out."

"Any news on Alvin's shoulder?" I swigged the beer to be sociable.

"Doc over at New Haven General says he's not as young as he used to be, but he'll be okay."

"What about Junior?"

"He'll probably get a few years in state prison. A couple bullets that hit the dancer and one of the patrons came from his gun."

I sipped and waited a second before I changed the subject. "The other day, you had some pretty hard words about Reacher. I've never met him. Anything else you can tell me for my background check would help."

She nodded a couple of times as if she was thinking things through. "At first, I liked him. He was straight with me. I had a young son at home and I was worried I might be left on the outside looking in after the big changes coming down because of the end of the Cold War."

"What did he say about that?" Gaspar asked.

"He told me not to worry. He said my son would be out of college before they figured out the force reduction. He was dead wrong, but it made me feel better at the time." She did seem to have liked Reacher, which stood in stark contrast to the impression she gave me in Tony Clifton's office.

She swigged her beer. Now that she'd started talking, she kept going. "We got along well enough. I brought him coffee. He had an emergency once and I loaned him all the money I had. I think it was about forty-seven dollars. He paid me back fifty-two, which included my babysitter."

She chuckled. She drained the beer and returned the bottle to the table.

I said, "Junior told me that Jack Reacher was the one who messed up Alvin's knee. Is that true?"

A dark cloud floated across her features. "Lucky for him I didn't know that until after he'd gone. Got off with a slap on the wrist for it, too." She scowled. The hard tone she'd used in Major Clifton's office that first day had returned, rocky as granite. "Just because he busted those officers, they let him off the hook for what he did to Alvin. A lot of us didn't think that was right at the time. Still don't."

The anger rolled off her in waves that I could feel like the pulsing of the loud country music in my veins. "What about Summer? What did she think about it?"

"She thought it was just fine. But then, she would. She was sleeping with Reacher and she thought he hung the moon. She made out like he was some kind of misunderstood hero or something." Jones's scowl grabbed tighter across her face. "If Summer hadn't spoken up for him, he'd have gone to Leavenworth for what he did. The pain he put Alvin through was criminal. Disabled a fine man who did nothing but take care of his own."

I nodded like what she'd said made perfect sense. "You heard about Colonel Summer's accident? The same night as the shooting."

"I heard."

"What do you think happened?"

"I told Sheriff Taylor. She was speeding around here in that little car like she always did. The truck slowed down and she didn't. Nasty way to go, but at least it was over quick. She wasn't disabled and in pain her whole life with a busted leg. Could've gone that way, you know." Jones's cold words made her sound a little sorry that Summer died instantly.

"What do you know about the dancer that was the catalyst for everything that happened here the other night?"

"Nothing much. She grew up around here, but she was a mousy little thing. High tailed it outta here with Mayne when she was too young to know better. She shouldn't have messed with Delta Force. Those guys are all a little crazy, you ask me." She drained her beer and set the bottle down. "Reacher's still causing trouble and he's been gone from around here for twenty years."

"What do you mean?"

"The shooter. Jeffrey Mayne. He and Reacher had a beef, too. Around the same time as everything else. Reacher shoved a bullet up Mayne's nose. Mayne didn't take that well at all. I wouldn't be surprised if they had another round or two before Reacher mustered out." She rolled her shoulders and her neck cracked. "Did some kind of permanent damage to Mayne's sinuses. Which got him discharged on a medical a couple of years later. After Mayne and Gloria were already gone from here." She shook her head and scowled darkly. "And now

Reacher circles back around and tears our lives up all over again—Alvin's bar all shot up, a bunch of people dead, Gloria included, Junior headed for the pen—"

"What do you mean? Reacher was here during the shooting?" I blinked. I felt whipsawed.

"I don't know where Reacher is, I told you that." Jones shrugged. "But whatever happened here that night, it's all because of him. Back in 1990, Reacher messed up Alvin's leg for life because he thought Alvin had knocked one of the dancers around. Wasn't true then and never been true since. Mayne thinking Alvin somehow kept Gloria away from him by force or something wasn't true, either. People think Alvin looks scary, so he must be scary, you know?"

Jones was drifting. I brought her back online: "So why did Reacher shove the bullet up Mayne's nose?"

"Mayne had delivered the bullet a couple of days before with Reacher's name on it."

"A threat? For what?"

"Reacher was poking into things he shouldn't have been, disrespecting a murdered officer. Delta guys didn't appreciate it, I guess." She stood and collected her empty beer bottle. Ours were still full, so she left them on the table. "I've gotta get back to work."

Gaspar said, "Did you know either one of the big rig drivers involved in that crash?"

"Sure. I know both of those men. Fine fathers and good truckers, too. This must be tearing them up."

"You heard about the deer, then?"

She nodded. "Deer on the road around here are pretty normal. We got farmers all over the place and the deer eat the crops. Oftentimes we've got goats and cows on the roads, too.

Natural hazards. Hell, there's even a couple of signs on both sides of the highway saying to watch out for them. Summer knew that, just like everybody else does."

I met her eyes with a steady gaze. "You didn't kill Summer, did you?"

I expected her to bridle at the question or be shocked by the idea that anything but Summer's own recklessness had killed her, but she just held my gaze and said, "Not me," smirking in a way that suggested she knew who did.

She wove through the tables and stopped to chat with a few of the men on her way back to the front. As I watched her go, I wondered if she'd had any sniper training and whether she'd qualified on the L115A3 rifle.

CHAPTER TWENTY-EIGHT

THE CROWDED, NOISY BAR provided as much cover from eavesdroppers as anywhere we could go, so I pulled out my secure cell and pushed the #1 speed dial button. When the Boss answered, I asked, "What is going on here?"

"It's classified." His voice was quiet. I could barely hear him through the bar's noise.

"What isn't?"

"Not much."

"I can ask Finlay."

"If you think he'll tell you, be my guest. I'd love to hear what he has to say."

I took a breath. Finlay and Cooper refused to be played off against each other and I should remember that. "The FBI is investigating Dynamic Defense Systems for what, exactly?"

"Can't say."

"Can't or won't?"

Silence.

"Who is investigating General Clifton? He's not within FBI jurisdiction. So it must be the Army's Inspector General. But what's the charge?" This one I already knew, but it was a test to see if he'd tell me.

"You should ask him."

Figures. "He knows he's being investigated?"

"Of course. Everybody knows."

That one surprised me. "Everybody?"

"It's impossible to keep a secret like that under wraps, even if they wanted to. The first thing they do is ask the General himself. You're a lawyer. You should understand the presumption of innocence. After that, they ask people around him who would know."

Now he was pissing me off. "Well if everybody knows, why not just tell us so we're in the loop like everyone else?"

"Where's the fun in that?" His tone wasn't jocular, though. I figured he didn't know everything, even though he wanted me to believe he did.

I took a long pull on the beer, which wasn't half bad, actually. I was feeling stubborn and belligerent and now I liked beer? Maybe my German DNA was more prominent than usual tonight. Dad would be happy.

"General Clifton is being investigated for some kind of corruption," I told him as if he didn't already know that much. "Corruption was Summer's specialty, so she was in the thick of it. Probably driving it. Jeffrey Mayne was also involved, somehow. He was Delta Force. Was he an Army trained sniper? And Thomas O'Connor is neck-deep in the whole thing."

"You always were a good guesser."

I took that as confirmation. "So what does any of this have to do with Reacher?"

"Have you seen him?"

"He hasn't walked up and introduced himself if that's what you're asking."

For the first time, his comeback wasn't quite so snappy. "Stay alert. He's not the kind of guy who talks much. He'll act first and sort later."

"He was one of the best snipers in the world at one time. Even if he's grown old and slow, he could still pull this one off, maybe. Did he shoot Summer?"

He paused. "Data downloaded from the satellites is inconclusive."

So he had something more from the satellites than the photos I'd seen from Sheriff Taylor. Maybe even photos of the sniper. "He's certainly capable."

He didn't deny the truth.

I said, "The shot wouldn't have been too difficult for him, back in the day, at least. Summer was speeding, but she was traveling at a steady pace along a well-marked and predictable roadway. Some calculations would have been required, but I heard from Joe Reacher's ex that Jack's always been good with numbers."

"This wasn't the world's longest or toughest sniper kill. Not even close."

"What was the world's longest sniper kill?" I asked.

"I haven't checked the record books lately, but last I heard, it was still 2.47 kilometers."

"Which is what?" I did a quick calculation in my head. "About a mile and a half? What kind of rifle? Accuracy International L115A3 Long-Range?"

"That's a reasonable choice."

Which meant yes. Lightweight, easy to transport, comes with a stand and a suppressor to reduce the noise and the flash.

I said, "It holds five rounds, too. Which means the shooter *could* get it wrong four times."

A team of FBI agents could comb the countryside out there and never find any evidence, though. Too much time had passed. Too much contamination of the scene from weather and travelers. And the terrain was rough. Mountains, trees, mud, and all manner of possible ways the evidence was probably destroyed.

The bullet that hit Summer was never going to surface, either, and for many of the same reasons.

"Expensive gun. Costs about $35,000." He paused. "Requires significant training to shoot, and a shooting range set up to handle practice with a gun like that."

I nodded, but I was fairly sure he couldn't see me. It was dark and smoky in here, for one thing. "It's portable, but probably about fifteen pounds for the weapon alone. That's pretty tough terrain out there. Any vehicles in the area at the time of the shot?"

"Not even any two-tracks to drive them on."

"You figure it couldn't have been a woman, then?"

"Not likely. We don't have very many female snipers in the modern military. And the military is the most likely place to train one."

"So he is a military-trained sniper with access to the best weapon for the job. He hiked into position, set up, shot to kill Summer, packed up, hiked out. And you never saw him and have no clue who he is."

"That about sums it up."

I said nothing.

After a long pause, he asked, "We're sure she was killed with a sniper shot?"

"The local medical examiner says she was. He showed us what he says is a bullet hole in her skull."

Another long pause. "You've seen plenty of bullet holes in skulls. Did it look like the real thing to you?"

I hesitated because, like I told Taylor, the bullet hole meant a premeditated kill of the coldest sort. Which was exactly the kind of thing Reacher *could* do. But it didn't sit well with me.

For one thing, this wasn't Reacher's style, was it? Everything I'd seen and heard about him indicated he was a guy who deployed direct physical confrontation instead of hiding in the trees to shoot a woman from a distance and slinking off afterward.

The most likely answer is usually the right one, though. Unless we could come up with a more likely expert marksman who had roamed freely around Fort Bird, the Boss would default to Reacher. And he'd probably be right.

At this point, we had a lot of questions and not many answers. We had seven bodies. A sniper. A bullet with Reacher's name on it. Finlay and Cooper still at war with each other for reasons neither would explain. And nobody was talking.

Which meant it was time to squeeze the most likely squawker.

CHAPTER TWENTY-NINE

THE UNRELENTING NOISE INSIDE *The Lucky Bar* was still the best place for conversation. I moved my chair closer to Gaspar and leaned in toward his ear. "Do you have brothers?"

He nodded and held up one index finger. "Paulo."

"Older or younger?"

"Younger by three years. You?"

I nodded and held up three fingers. "Older. Sisters?"

"Consuelo, Connie. Younger by five years. You?"

"One. Younger. Are you all protective of each other?"

"Very. You?"

I nodded, stood and waved him to his feet. "Let's go."

He followed me outside. The noise was still loud enough to cover conversation for another twenty yards, almost all the way to where he'd parked the Crown Vic. "Where are we going?"

"Fort Bird. We need some answers, don't you think?"

"Tony Clifton is in a tough position here. You wouldn't turn on your brothers, would you, Helga?"

I said nothing. Because it wouldn't be easy to overlook the high level corruption and murder that was going on here, even if one of my brothers was responsible and even if bringing him to justice would break my mother's heart.

Gaspar assumed the driving duties as usual. He took the county road this time because he hadn't driven the route that would have been Reacher's only choice back then and because we were in no hurry. About five miles down the road, he asked, "What did the Boss have to say?"

I shrugged. "The usual nothing. He figures the sniper is military trained. He's got satellite photos of the guy. He doesn't think it was Reacher, but he can't tell. Probably because the guy's covered from head to toe and as well camouflaged as the Army's woodland ACUs can make him."

Gaspar's eyebrows raised and he glanced toward me. "He told you that?"

"Not in so many words. He asked me if I'd seen Reacher. I took that to mean that he hadn't. And he was disappointed."

"Any clue what we're doing here yet?"

"Just guesses."

"Care to enlighten me?"

"I really wish I could. What do you think is going on?" I asked, more to let him talk than because I expected any flashes of brilliance. If he'd known anything brilliant, he'd have told me already.

Gaspar started with Fort Bird, where everything seemed to have started long ago, too. "Major Tony Clifton is using you. We can agree on that much, I assume."

I nodded. "For what, though?"

Gaspar ticked off the list. "He knows his brother is being investigated for corruption. He knew Summer was doing the investigating. He knows about the Reacher connections between them all."

I nodded. "Is Tony sending me after his brother because he's trying to sink Matthew Clifton or save him?"

Gaspar's eyebrows shot up. "Why would Tony Clifton think you could do either one?"

"What if he suspected that our Reacher file assignment is a ruse? The assignment does sound lame." Because the only explanation we had to offer was a lie. Lies were always lame.

"Can't argue with that."

"Maybe he thought I was really meeting with Summer about the corruption case against his brother."

Gaspar said, "That's a reasonable assumption. The FBI was involved in a parallel investigation to Summer's investigation into Matthew Clifton."

"Yes, and that one resulted in a prison sentence for General Clifton's classmate. Thomas O'Connor confirmed that."

"Stands to reason that Matthew Clifton is next."

"Okay. But either way, Tony Clifton had to have been relieved when Summer didn't show up for your meeting, right? Because Summer's prying and prodding and looking under rocks had been postponed a little while."

I nodded. "Makes sense."

"So why did he send you directly to Joe Reacher's ex-wife, Lesley Browning? When he did that, he had to know you'd end up right in the thick of Summer's investigation because of her husband's involvement. Why would Tony want you to pick up where Summer dropped off?"

I shook my head. These questions had been giving me a stomachache since Summer no-showed on my first trip to Fort Bird. Gaspar was my secret weapon. He thought the way Reacher thought. It didn't make me feel better to know that Gaspar had no answers, either.

Gaspar tapped his thumb on the steering wheel, thinking. "Did the Boss tell you the particulars of the corruption claims against General Clifton?"

I glared at him. Stupid question.

"Then why not call your pal Finlay and ask? He'd be delighted to be on your good side. Call him on the Boss's phone so he's sure to hear whatever Finlay says, too. That'll piss him off."

"Men are weird," I said and he laughed. I pulled out the Boss's phone and dialed Finlay's private number. The one on the card he'd given me the first night we met. When he answered, I skipped the pleasantries. "Why is General Matthew Clifton being investigated by the Inspector General?"

"Cooper does enjoy leaving you in the dark and watching you claw your way out, doesn't he?" The smirk in his voice probably matched the one on his face.

"Just answer the question."

"Rumor is that he's a little too close to his friends. He's confused. He thinks he's a politician instead of a General."

"You'd think he'd know the difference. Generals are warriors. Politicians are a bunch of liars." Cheeky, but I wasn't kidding.

Finlay, the consummate politician who reported to the most important politician in the world, laughed. "General Clifton has been granting defense contracts to his old West Point classmates on a no-bid basis. Cronyism is an illegal violation of policy. He knows it. He's been warned. And a couple of months ago, the FBI completed an investigation into one of his classmates, a retired Colonel now working for a defense contractor, which resulted in a conviction and a two-year jail sentence for taking kickbacks that O'Connor told you about."

"O'Connor didn't tell me that. All he said was ethics violations. Clifton is taking kickbacks?"

"We don't think so. But the jury's still out on that."

"What's his excuse? These guys always have a justification of some kind."

"He hasn't said for the record. But privately, he thinks the Army's being gutted by a bunch of politicians who want the military to save the world and do it on a puny budget that will get his soldiers killed."

"Can't argue with that," I said.

"Priorities, Otto. We're not made of money. We have budgets and we have to make hard choices sometimes."

"Oh, I see. Hiring another twelve staffers for a Senator is more important than keeping soldiers alive who are willing to put their boots on the ground. Sending a bunch of Secret Service dudes to a Brazil brothel is a wise use of money, too. Oh, all that wasted foreign aid food and drugs rotting in the sunshine in Africa? Perfect thing to do with the budget. Let's print more money to do all of that. I get it, Finlay."

"I don't think you do." Now his tone was steel. "I'm doing you a favor here. You asked me. I'm telling you what you don't know and apparently can't find out." He paused for an audible deep breath. "It's not smart to bite the hand that feeds you, Otto. You'd do well to remember that."

What I heard next was nothing but dead air, but I imagined I could hear the Boss laughing his ass off. Which did nothing to help my mood.

I dropped the secure cell into my pocket. Fort Bird was four miles ahead, according to the GPS in the Crown Vic, so I made the report of the conversation succinct: "The Army is making an example of General Clifton and he doesn't like it."

Gaspar rubbed his palm over his face and groaned. "God, I hate sanctimonious jerks. Why can't people just do what they're supposed to do for once?"

"If they did, Chico, we'd be out of a job."

"I guess that means Finlay didn't tell you who killed Summer, either."

"Crap. He pissed me off and I forgot to ask."

The Boss's secure cell vibrated in my pocket and I almost ignored it. But this time, I fished it out and answered. "Otto."

"He's not there. You're wasting time."

He meant Tony Clifton. The Boss always knew where we were going and why. "Where is he, then?"

"Fort Herald. Tickets waiting for you at the airport. Get out there while there's still time."

"Only if you tell me who killed Eunice Summer."

His silence was total, but he didn't hang up. It wasn't the first time I'd been insubordinate. And it wouldn't be the last, the way this assignment was going. But I wasn't planning to walk into an ambush without at least one solid answer to something important that I wanted to know.

Finally, he said, "I'll send you the satellite images. You tell me."

Once again, I was holding a phone full of nothing but dead air.

Gaspar laughed out loud and I threw the phone at him. He ducked. The phone hit the window and bounced onto his lap. "Come on, Sunshine. You know we're going to Fort Herald either way."

"He knows who killed Summer. They both do."

"Of course they do. But that's not the point, is it?"

I hated it when he was right. "Don't you ever get tired of being used, Chico?"

He shrugged and handed me the phone. "I've got four going on five kids and twenty years to go. Hello. I follow orders. What's your excuse?"

His comment triggered a synapse in my brain or something like a lightning flash. I sat up straighter in the seat and turned to face Gaspar. "Remember I told you to concentrate on how they killed Summer?"

He scowled. "I'm not senile."

"Think about it." I gave him a hand. "The sniper knows Summer's on her way to Fort Bird. He knows why she's coming to Fort Bird. He knows the route she's taking. He knows approximately when she'll pass mile marker #224. He's in place and set up. He's had time to adjust for all variables. He's as ready as he's going to get. The conditions aren't perfect, but they never are."

Gaspar nodded. "With you so far."

"The shot's not impossible, obviously, because he made it."

"But he could easily have missed. The traffic cams were out so he couldn't see her coming. He was a long distance from the kill zone and she was traveling eighty miles an hour." He glanced my way. "Why didn't he miss?"

I waited half a moment to be sure he was paying attention. "He didn't miss because he knew *precisely* when to shoot."

Gaspar scowled again. "How the hell could he have known that?"

"He knew because Summer told him."

He looked as shocked as if a yeti had jumped out of nowhere and landed in the Crown Vic on the seat between us. "What?"

"Summer called me from the car on the way to Fort Bird, remember? She told me she was driving and where. She told me what time she'd meet me. She was the only person who knew that information." My guess about the rest wasn't much of a stretch. "I'm betting Summer called him, too. Or maybe he called her. Either way, she told him where she was and when she'd be at mile marker #224. She was talking to him. At the precise moment, he shot and killed her."

"So he knew exactly when she'd be within his kill zone because she told him while it was happening." Gaspar said nothing for a moment and then nodded. A grin broke out that lit up his face. "That's brilliant."

I said, "When we check her cell phone data, we'll confirm the call."

Gaspar nodded. "And identify the guy she talked to."

"Doubtful. He's not dumb enough to have used a traceable phone. Finlay or the Boss can find the number, but that phone is long gone." I shook my head. "The only way we might do it is through voice comparisons. There's no question that the call was recorded by the Boss or Finlay or the phone company or someone. Everything is recorded these days. And both Finlay and the Boss were watching Summer. They would have been recording her, too."

"What about the truckers?" Gaspar asked after a bit. "Too convenient, it seems to me, that a couple of phantom deer dashed across the road in exactly that spot at exactly that time. Were they in place to slow Summer down, just in case he missed with the first shot and needed a second?"

"Possible. But you heard Dr. Smith. She was already dead before she hit the tanker."

"The truckers didn't manage to kill her, so their part in this mess gets ignored? No harm, no foul?" He glanced at me. "That's not usually your style."

Definitely not even close to my style. "Jones said the truckers are decent men. So we'll find out how decent they are when we bring them in for questioning."

"They might have meant to kill her. Or not." Gaspar set the cruise control and stretched his right leg. "Could go either way."

"We still need to know who the shooter is and why he did it. Something tells me Tony Clifton can help with that." I stretched my neck again. "The Boss wouldn't be sending us to Fort Herald again otherwise."

"Can't argue with that logic, either."

Maybe not, but the scowl on his face told me precisely what he thought. He needed the paycheck, but he didn't have to like what came next.

CHAPTER THIRTY

THIS TIME, WE ARRIVED at the Fort Herald main gate with nothing but Gaspar's veteran's card paving the way, unless the Boss had worked his magic. There were several cars and trucks in front of us. When we reached the gate, the sentry said, "Headed to the shooting demonstrations?"

Shooting demonstrations? Sure. Why not.

Gaspar said, "Yep."

"You know where it is? Just follow those vehicles ahead of you. Can't possibly miss the noise."

"Will do."

The sentry handed Gaspar a generic visitor pass and waved us through. Instead of following the crowd, we drove to General Matthew Clifton's office building, as we had before. No one stopped us on the way.

When we arrived and parked and went inside, Gaspar asked for General Clifton. "He's at Range Foxtrot. Our newest graduating class is performing training demonstrations out there with the Marksmanship Unit."

"Is Major Anthony Clifton here?" I asked since it was Tony I wanted to question first.

"Haven't seen him."

Something about the setup felt wrong. "Are training demonstrations usually held here?"

"Ma'am?"

"I thought the Army's sniper training school was at Fort Benning, Georgia."

"Yes, Ma'am. But the U.S. Army Marksmanship Unit performs demonstrations and competes around the world, including in the Olympics." He shrugged and shook his head. "Our new soldiers appreciate the opportunity to learn from the best. We invite certain civilians every year. After the demonstrations, there will be a train-the-trainer clinic. The General is likely to be out there pretty late."

We returned to the Crown Vic and I pulled up a map of Fort Herald. Range F was about two miles south. Gaspar pointed the Crown Vic in the right direction and drove the speed limit the whole way. No one tried to stop us.

"Did you ever perform any kind of shooting demonstration for civilian visitors when you were in the Army?" I asked.

"I wasn't a member of the Marksmanship Unit. It's an elite team. Stiff competition." He paused. "But the world has changed. It's all about PR now. These days, the Unit probably has a Facebook page."

At the range, the parking lot was full. Presumably vehicles belonging to visitors observing the demonstrations. Family members and soldiers and a few officers, probably. The two types were easily distinguishable by their clothing. Anybody on active duty wore ACUs. The rest of us were dressed like civilians.

Gaspar found an empty bit of grass at the far edge of the parking area and nosed the Crown Vic into the open space. We hopped out and rushed as quickly as we could to the visitor viewing area.

The range was a large, rectangular open field. We parked on the south side and walked north toward the visitor viewing area, which was roped off to separate visitors from military personnel. If the setup had been a football field, we'd have parked in the end zone. The visitors would have been confined by the ropes behind the ten-yard line.

There were about thirty soldiers with various weapons milling around the shooting areas inside the ropes. Targets were spaced out in the field at well-marked distances near the opposite end zone. Sidelines of demarcation were seven-foot hay bale stacks on either side of the open field where live rounds would be fired.

Most spectators wore ear protection and a few didn't, which was probably a violation of some regulation or another. Those of us without the bulky sound and shock-absorbing earphones were in danger of significant hearing damage, if not immediate and lasting deafness. There was probably a station to collect ear protection, but I didn't see it. We'd have to make do with jamming our fingers in our ears.

The entire process was carefully structured. Certain soldiers shot certain weapons in a certain order for a certain number of rounds like an elaborately choreographed ballet. My FBI training had included operations exactly like this, minus the visitors.

The demonstrations moved smoothly and without fanfare. Soldiers lined up at the front of the range near the twenty-yard line, each holding the same weapon. Targets were lined up at the back of the range. When orders were shouted over the megaphone and repeated through loudspeakers, soldiers shot at the targets. After a few rounds, the line of soldiers changed and the weapons changed and the shooting recommenced.

The noise level made communication with Gaspar difficult. I touched his arm and pointed to indicate where he should search and where I would.

General Clifton's ACUs blended in with everyone else's and it took me a minute to spot him on a covered, elevated platform erected on the east side high enough to see over the hay bale sideline observing the soldiers on the range. Standing next to General Clifton on his left side was his brother, Tony. An officer holding a megaphone and shouting instructions stood on General Clifton's right side. Perhaps the instructions came from General Clifton, but it was impossible to say from this distance.

The megaphone distorted the officer's halting delivery, but something about it was familiar. I'd heard it before. But I couldn't place it.

Gaspar had moved a dozen yards away. When I captured his attention, we each headed for General Clifton's position, weaving between the others milling around inside and outside the restricted visitor's area. Gaspar kept up as well as he could, but the gap between us seemed to grow.

The closer I got to the stage, the more familiar the megaphone voice sounded. And I saw another man I recognized on the platform, too. Standing slightly behind and to the left of General Clifton. Thomas O'Connor, compliance officer for Dynamic Defense Systems and current husband of Joe Reacher's ex-wife.

The gang was all here. Exactly as the Boss had orchestrated, no doubt. But I still couldn't fathom why.

When I'd moved to within twenty yards of him, something

drew General Clifton's attention my way. He turned his head toward me and his gaze met mine across the distance. He stared at me as if he couldn't believe I was there, walking toward him. Which I wasn't. I was walking toward Tony.

Then he bent his head to say something to the officer with the megaphone. He also said something to his brother and something to Thomas O'Connor. After that, he turned and moved in the opposite direction.

It was the last straw. I was done with this cat-and-mouse crap. Anyone in that big a hurry to dodge me was clearly worth chasing. Somebody was going to tell me what was going on here, and if I couldn't get it out of the Boss or Finlay, then I'd go straight to the General's mouth.

He hurried off the platform and down on the north side. He made better headway than we did. Crowds on our side of the stage were thick while those on his side were nearly nonexistent. I saw his head bouncing above the heads of the spectators on my side with each step, which made it easier to ghost him. He couldn't see me through the crowds while he might have seen the taller Gaspar.

I looked back and found Gaspar, his progress was slowed by his gimpy leg. He cocked his head to signal that he saw me looking at him. I waved my arm to signal moving to the right and turned to weave through the crowd in that direction. I broke through the edge of the viewers and trotted around the periphery of the stage, moving steadily toward the general's side.

General Clifton had three advantages. He'd managed a significant head start and his legs were a lot longer than mine, which accelerated his ground speed. Those were obstacles I could overcome. His biggest advantage was that he knew the terrain and I did not, and that wasn't an obstacle I could leap across.

I pushed a little harder, striving to close the gap, but the distance between us widened. I was breathing harder than I should have been when I reached the empty stretch of the field on the other side of the platform. But I could see General Clifton clearly ahead of me now, headed north, toward the far end of the field.

The voice of the officer with the megaphone continued to nag me every time he shouted halting instructions to the soldiers in the shooting area, but I was focused on my quarry. Which was why I didn't see Tony leave the stage and follow behind me. Gaspar might have tried to warn me, but I couldn't possibly have heard him over the shooting and the cheering crowds and the distance.

General Clifton traveled along the hay bale partition, the only thing separating the live rounds shooting down the range on the west side from the open field on the east side. The hay bale fence ended about twenty yards ahead of him. When he reached the end, he stopped and turned to face me.

The rhythmic shooting continued. I glanced back. The stationary row of soldiers at the south end of the range commenced fire again toward the north end. I felt like I was running at slow speed along with the zipping bullets.

At this distance, the gunfire was slightly quieter. The intermittent rounds hit their targets ahead of me on the other side of the hay bales with a frequency that sounded like ten-pound popcorn exploding against a heavy gauge steel popper.

General Clifton waited at the end of the bales until I was within mutual shouting distance. He stood with both feet firmly planted shoulder-width apart, hands clasped behind his back. He allowed me to approach five yards closer before he held up his left hand, palm out.

I stopped. He lowered his left hand and it joined his right hand behind his back, which made me nervous.

My weapon was holstered. But so was his.

"Reacher isn't worth it, you know," he said, his voice barely carrying across the distance when spaced between the still-deafening rounds. "When you find him, he'll be uncontrollable. Like he was when we discharged him. Like he was in 1990, when he and Summer decided to change the world. Like he was at West Point before that. Like he's always been."

"Not my issue, General. I don't need to control Reacher. I'm only building the file."

"And I'm only standing here for a chat." He sneered. "Did you imagine you'd arrest me? Put handcuffs on me out here in front of my men?"

Arrest him? For what? "We could have a quieter chat somewhere else."

"Did Cooper tell you what happened to Colonel Willard?" He cocked his head and bared his teeth in a feral smile. The exploding ten-pound popcorn sounds came again, this time in more frequent bursts of several shots at a time. The shooters had changed to firing different weapons.

Willard. I didn't recognize the name. I'd met a lot of soldiers and I was hyper-focused on Clifton. "I don't know Colonel Willard. Who is he?"

"He *was* a man who followed orders. Orders Reacher didn't like. Ask Cooper. Or Finlay. Either one can tell you." Clifton's cold eyes and hard jaw telegraphed his contempt even from that distance. "They should have told you before they sent you into the field on this one, Otto."

"What does Willard have to do with my assignment?"

I was barely listening. My mind was engaged in a

complicated assessment of multiple variables surrounding our standoff. If he made a move for his weapon—which, for whatever reason, seemed entirely possible—I could shoot Clifton. Disable him, maybe. Likely my best option. It would work as long as he didn't shoot me first.

But otherwise, he'd win any physical contest between us. If I could keep him talking until Gaspar arrived, we might do together what I wasn't physically big enough or strong enough to do alone.

And I was still nervous about what he might be holding behind his back.

CHAPTER THIRTY-ONE

CLIFTON'S STANCE WAS STIFF, wide, unwavering. "This is your fault, Otto. As much as Cooper's and Finlay's. Just remember that. You should have refused."

"Refused what?" I asked.

He glanced above my head and his eyes widened before he yelled, "Tony! Halt!"

I whipped my head around and saw Tony Clifton five yards behind me. He'd stopped, mid-stride, as ordered, staring beseechingly at his brother. In a flash, I drew my weapon and turned toward General Clifton again.

He stood as ramrod straight as he'd been taught in basic training all those years ago and tossed us a quick left-handed salute.

I thought for a split second that things might work out okay.

Everything happened swiftly and simultaneously after that as if Clifton had been waiting for a signal.

First, the megaphone voice rang out with new orders to fire. Multiple rounds hit their targets. The audience applauded and cheered and more rounds were fired.

My hearing was overwhelmed with so much noise that the surreal effect was one of hearing nothing at all.

General Clifton drew his right hand around from back to front at his waist and showed the grenade he'd been holding. Then he sidestepped to his right and moved fluidly to the other side of the fence. The live fire side.

I ran full out down the remaining length of the hay bale line toward General Clifton. Tony Clifton's boots pounded the ground behind me.

When I reached the end and could see around the hay bales into the open shooting range, General Clifton was already ten feet away. I couldn't reach him without running into the line of live fire.

I shouted, "Get the hell back here!"

Tony yelled, "Matt! Matt!"

But he ran in the opposite direction. Along the back of the row of targets. Live rounds were landing solidly as they were aimed by the highly qualified soldiers who didn't expect Clifton to be behind the targets.

He was hit by the bullets passing through their targets and was bleeding, but he kept upright on his feet, staggering a few more steps.

He turned and looked at me and raised his left hand to his mouth, fingers bunched, and blew me a kiss as if to say, "Kiss off!"

Tony grabbed my arm. His rigid posture held us both anchored to the dirt.

A sudden coldness hit me like a sucker punch to my stomach. Cold radiated through my limbs.

As we watched wide-eyed, mouths gaping, his brother waited briefly for the rapid shooting frequency to commence, then slipped between the targets from the back to the front and stood directly facing the line of fire.

The man with the megaphone didn't start to yell for what felt like a solid hour.

"Hold your fire! Hold your fire!" he finally screamed over and over into the megaphone. The orders were picked up by a microphone somewhere and squealed out from loudspeakers around the periphery of the range, the parking lot, the crowds.

But it was far too late.

General Matthew Clifton's body had jerked and twitched and bounced with the impact of at least a dozen rounds in a macabre dance like a marionette controlled by a puppeteer having a seizure.

As he fell to the ground, he opened his right hand and dropped the grenade.

I dove behind the hay bales, slammed prone to the ground and covered my head with both arms. Tony Clifton did the same.

The grenade exploded.

I felt the earth move under my belly and my body lifted off the ground and slammed back, hard. Dirt and debris were thrown into the air with great force. On the way back down, clods and rocks and sticks pelted my body for what seemed like a full minute or more.

When the shooting finally stopped and the debris finally settled, I felt all of my limbs to be sure nothing was broken. Then I crawled to the edge of the fence and lifted my head and looked onto the open shooting range.

General Clifton was twisted into an odd position on the ground. Blood stained his uniform. His right leg and left arm had been separated from his torso. Dead eyes stared across the open ground directly at me.

A hand landed on my shoulder from behind. Instinct took over. I jumped straight up in the air and turned around with my gun leveled center mass.

Gaspar knocked the gun aside before I could shoot him. Thank God.

Tony Clifton had risen to his hands and knees. Wide eyes stared at his brother's mutilated and bloody corpse. Tears coursed down his filthy face. He didn't seem to notice.

I turned again to see the identifiable parts of General Matthew Clifton's body on the ground in pools of blood and riddled with gunshots. Strangely, his head was intact and except for the dirt and sweat, his face seemed almost the same as it had in life. His expression was frozen in death and not the least bit horrified.

The shooting and the megaphone and the sound system and all other noises had stopped. An unnatural quiet surrounded everything. Or maybe my ears were damaged beyond the ability to hear what noises existed.

But in the silence I realized the owner of the distorted voice behind the megaphone.

I grabbed Gaspar's arm and pulled him aside. He bent his head to hear me. "I know who killed Summer. And I know why."

CHAPTER THIRTY-TWO

"HOW IS THE ARMY explaining the incident?" Gaspar asked as we settled into the visitor chairs in Reacher's old office at Fort Bird.

Major Tony Clifton's once handsome face was gray and haggard. He'd aged two decades since we'd seen him last. The charming lines around his expressive eyes were deeper. He was wrung out and he looked it.

"Training accident. That's all anyone needs to know." He was seated across the desk. An untouched mug of coffee rested near his phone. He hadn't offered us coffee today and no one brought any. "That's how Matt wanted it."

Gaspar shrugged, but I lowered my gaze.

General Clifton's dress uniform had been tiled with every medal there was. He'd excelled in combat and in peacetime. He was as strong as any human could be, mentally and physically. He'd attended dozens of similar demonstrations and he knew the safe places as well as the unsafe ones. No one who knew General Matthew Clifton would believe he'd simply wandered into the line of fire and been riddled with bullets.

But even if people wanted to believe his death was an accident, one look at the body would've proven otherwise. The bullets alone wouldn't have ripped his body apart like that grenade did.

"I'm sorry, Tony," I said. If his family was okay with calling his suicide a training accident, I wouldn't be the one to clear the record. "He wouldn't have been sent to prison. He'd have received a suspended sentence, at the very most. There's precedent for that and he certainly didn't deserve worse."

There was no evidence that the West Point friends he'd awarded the no-bid defense contracts to, like Thomas O'Connor, were less than the best contractors for the job. No evidence of kickbacks or overcharging. Everything I'd read about the new drones his cronies had presented was glowingly positive and the budget was strictly adhered to. In fact, it looked like O'Connor's firm would bring the project in under budget. What General Matthew Clifton had done with the no-bid contracts was unethical, but the results had nonetheless been a rousing success by all accounts.

"He got the news the day before. Summer's investigation had already resulted in charges against other officers. Matt knew what was coming. He knew the shitstorm that was coming his way and he refused to be subjected to it." Tony's shoulders sagged and his voice thickened. "He'd devoted his life to the Army. He should have been promoted this week to a three-star. He was headed to the Joint Chiefs. He simply wouldn't accept anything less."

"I'm sorry," I said again because I had nothing more brilliant to offer.

He ran a flat palm across his face. "Matt didn't have it in him to accept a reprimand or a demotion or be forced to retire or face disgrace. He really felt death was his only choice."

In his shoes, I'm not sure I'd have had the courage to do what Clifton did, but I understood it. Soldiers and FBI agents, too, knew there were worse things than dying. "You discussed the matter with him, then?"

"Several times. I argued with him until I was hoarse. We worked behind the scenes to change the outcome, too." He paused and looked at me directly and nodded slowly. "That's why I sent you to Joe Reacher's ex. Leslie Browning. I knew that would get you to her husband and Dynamic Defense Systems. You'd investigate independently and find out there was no harm, no foul. In fact, Matt got the Army a better result than we'd have managed any other way. His solution was expedient, too. He thought that should be enough. He thought the Inspector General would do the right thing, in the end. But that didn't happen."

"Rules are rules, Tony," Gaspar said. "Every soldier knows that. Surely Matt must've."

Tony hung his head. After a moment, he squared his shoulders and looked at me again as if he'd mentally turned a corner of some kind, determined to carry on. "I'm sure you didn't come all the way back here to Bird to offer your condolences. How can I be of assistance to the FBI today?"

Quick jolts of electricity ran through me. Those were the exact words I'd heard from Thomas O'Connor, too. The echo effect was eerie.

"Sheriff Taylor has a BOLO out on your Sergeant Church. We wanted to give you a heads up." Taylor's "Be On the Lookout" order had gone out an hour ago. He might have already found Church unless Church was on base. "Come into New Haven with us to observe the interrogation. You know Church better than any of the rest of us. Taylor could use your input."

"On what charge?" Tony's eyebrows shot north. Both of them at the same time. He leveled a glassy stare in our direction. "Sheriff Taylor has no jurisdiction over our soldiers. Neither do you."

"The homicide was a shooting off the base," Gaspar informed him. "The case is Sheriff Taylor's bailiwick." Gaspar didn't mention that we were the ones who put the evidence in Taylor's hands to support the arrest.

Tony's response was quick and sharp. "Is this about the incident at *The Lucky Bar* the other night? Because Church wasn't even there. He was with me."

I leaned in and asked calmly, "What do you know about Sergeant Church's integrity, Tony?"

Major Clifton leaned back and crossed his legs. "As much as I need to know. He's Army. That makes him one of ours."

"You know he's a trained sniper, right?"

His curt nod gave no quarter. "Damned good one. Two tours in Iraq. More than three dozen confirmed kills. Member of the Marksmanship Unit for a while, too." If the mention of this particular unit caused him any trouble so soon after watching his brother die at the unit's hand, he gave no sign of it.

I pressed on, undaunted. "That's a lot of expensive Army resources spent on Church. Why was he sitting at that desk out there bringing your coffee the day I arrived?"

"I told you when you asked me the first time. An informal disciplinary issue with tardiness two days in a row. That's all. I didn't even make a note in his file. Just between him and me." He raised his hand and flipped his fingers as if to dust me off. Then he raised his coffee cup. "You notice he's not sitting out there and bringing you coffee today."

I nodded. That's what I remembered about him. Church was late. Two days in a row.

Which made sense. The Boss had set up my appointment at the last minute. Church must have learned that Summer would be driving down the Interstate to Fort Bird from Rock Creek. He probably knew her appointment was with me and he knew why. Tony Clifton might even have told him.

So the first day, Church was late because he was scouting the sniper's nest. Finding the right spot to lie in wait for Summer. Judging the terrain, the wind direction, the difficulty of the shot. Maybe he even took a few practice shots, although that might have been too risky. I made a mental note to ask Sheriff Taylor if anyone had reported damage that might have come from practice rounds.

The second day, I figured Church was late because instead of coming to work, he'd gone to his nest and lay in wait until Summer drove past, and then he killed her.

When I saw Church limping that day in the Officers Club, it might have been because he'd pulled a muscle or something. The terrain was rough out there. He'd have been in a hurry to get back to Bird before I arrived for my appointment with Summer.

The scenario was more than plausible.

"Surely you don't get involved whenever a soldier has a minor issue with his boss," I said. "Why did you take such a personal interest in Sergeant Church?"

Tony cleared his throat and shrugged. "Matthew asked me to look after him."

I leaned in further. "Why?"

"Church's father had been a friend of Matt's. Matt never married and had no kids of his own. Like me, he was married to the Army. So when Church's father died, Matt took an interest in the boy." He cleared his throat again and glanced down briefly to blink. "I guess Matt was the father Church never had."

This next bit was tricky. I'd gone over it in my head a few times, but subjects don't always respond the way I imagine they will. To change the dynamic slightly, I sniffed the air and pretended to notice the aroma.

I nodded toward his mug. "Any chance we can get some of that great coffee? Who knows when we'll get another opportunity?"

Tony stood and left the room without a word.

CHAPTER THIRTY-THREE

HE CAME BACK WITH three mugs and placed them on the desk like Sergeant Church had done that first day. I remembered Church had seemed annoyed at his post. His hair had been wet, too. Why hadn't I noticed that? Because it didn't matter so much at the time.

While Tony resettled on the other side of the desk, we picked up our mugs and I sipped mine. Gaspar held his and didn't drink because Tony hadn't mixed a gallon of milk and a cup full of sugar into it.

"Thank you." The coffee here really was outstanding. Drinking it was no chore at all. "You mentioned Church's father when I was here before. Said his dad had been the CO of the 110th for a while. Reacher's Special Investigations unit. Remember that?"

Tony nodded.

"Well, I checked the records. There was never a CO named Church, according to the Army."

His eyes widened and he gave his head a couple of vigorous shakes. "Of course there was. Matt knew him. They served in Armored Division together. I already told you that."

"I did some more checking and I found out that Sergeant James Church's name was changed when he was about five years old." I settled back in my chair and propped my elbows on the chair arms. "His parents had a nasty divorce. His mother changed back to her maiden name and changed the boy's name, too. As if to erase all traces of his father."

Gaspar had pushed his chair back and extended his legs, crossed at the ankles, and folded his hands in his lap. He looked completely relaxed. "Guy must have been a total jerk for her to do that, don't you think?"

Tony shrugged. "Matt said he was a difficult guy. Not well liked. But he did the job and followed his orders."

I relaxed further into my chair as if we were chatting about nothing important. "I noticed where Church was when General Clifton died. Did you?"

Tony nodded. "He was standing right next to me on the platform. He was on the megaphone, handling the demonstrations. Why?"

"He lives off post, I'm told. Where is he right now?" I glanced out the window, where the winter sun cast an orange glow over the pines.

He shrugged and drank his coffee. "I'm not his CO. On base somewhere, I guess. Where else would he be?"

"Call him in here. Let's see if we're mistaken." I looked back at Tony and offered a slow smile. "If we're wrong, we can clear everything up and I'll take all of the heat."

He paused briefly before he picked up the phone and asked an MP to find Sergeant Church. "What do you think he's done?"

"Before we left Fort Herald, we asked the Provost to pull the sentry logs for November 19, the day of Summer's death. We've been looking through them for the past half hour. The logs confirm that Church logged out at 0710 and returned at 1030 hours." I watched for a dawning recognition, but it didn't come. "Eyewitnesses put Summer's time of death at approximately 0930. During Church's absence."

He stared at me as if I'd suddenly sprouted horns. "You think *Church* killed Colonel Summer? What possible motive would he have to do that? He didn't even know her."

"Maybe. Maybe not." I stood. "But he knew she was about to ruin General Clifton, didn't he? He knew about her investigation and he knew she was the one who was pushing for his prosecution. She wanted General Clifton court-martialed and sent to Leavenworth, didn't she?"

He flinched back. He seemed simply bewildered now. He rubbed the base of his neck. "That was her job. You said yourself that she wasn't necessarily going to win that battle."

I paced the small room, between the door and Gaspar's chair. "The night of the shooting at *The Lucky Bar*, I told you all three of the day's events were related. You said I was wrong."

"I remember."

"We were both wrong. I didn't know enough about Summer's work then. I thought the connections were all about Reacher."

"Reacher?" He looked like he was staring into a lighted refrigerator in the middle of the dark night.

"Reacher was here for nineteen days. He touched every single person involved in this mess. Everybody from Alvin Barry to Madeline Jones to Jeffrey Mayne and more." I stopped pacing and clasped my hands behind my back. "*Everybody* had some sort of beef with Reacher. The common link, I thought, was Jack Reacher."

Tony frowned and pursed his lips for a second before he said, "Reacher hasn't been here in twenty years."

"We don't know that for sure, do we? The truth is, nobody seems to know where Reacher is. And that's the problem."

He shook his head as if to clear it of sludge that clouded his brain. "Why on earth would any of these people care?"

"Now you're getting to the heart of it. First, let's assume somebody wanted to lure Reacher back to Fort Bird. How would they do it?"

Major Clifton lifted his shoulders and raised both hands, palms up.

"One thing about Reacher is crystal clear," I told him. "Every person we've interviewed has said a version of the same thing. Even you."

"What?"

"The Reacher brothers, Jack and Joe, were like clones. They looked alike. They talked alike. What did Matthew say about Joe? He was a hell of a guy. Both Reachers were intensely loyal. They took care of their friends. They did the right thing."

He nodded with every sentence as I laid it out. "Yeah, so?"

"Reacher would come back to Fort Bird if he knew his friends were in trouble. He would do the right thing, no matter what the cost."

"What's your point?"

"So what do you think Reacher would do if he found out a guy had killed one of his very close friends? A woman whose only goal in all of this was to do the right thing? A woman Reacher was having an affair with back in 1990?"

"Probably the same thing I would do. The same thing Joe would have done. He'd come and kill the son of a bitch."

I nodded. If you knew anything at all about Jack Reacher, the logic was flawless.

"You're saying Reacher and Summer were colleagues and lovers? That Church found out? And Church killed Summer to lure Reacher here?" Tony had set his mug on the desk and leaned on both forearms.

"And also because Church wanted to prevent Summer from hurting Matthew," Gaspar added. "In his book, she was a hypocrite. She'd been AWOL with Reacher back then and they'd stolen Army vouchers to finance a little fling in Paris. Church must have felt she was corrupt and she sat in judgment of General Clifton, a man he admired like a father."

Tony shook his head and sat back in his chair. "That's crazy. Can you prove any of it?"

"Won't have to," I said. "Church will confess. He's proud of what he's done. And he'll be prouder still if he can get Reacher to show his face back here before Taylor arrests him."

"Why the hell would he want Reacher to come back here so badly?" Tony continued shaking his head as if he couldn't make the marbles roll down the chutes inside his skull.

"That was the question I wrestled with, too," I replied, sitting back with my coffee again to give him a little more space. "But Matthew told me before he died."

The mention of his brother's death stilled Tony. He'd latched onto the Church problem as a distraction, maybe. Bringing Matthew back to the front of his mind snapped his attention to sharp focus on his loss again.

"Matthew said Church's father was a man who followed orders," I explained. "But like I told you, his name wasn't

Church. His name was Willard. His last tour was CO of the 110th Special Operations Unit. Reacher's unit. Do you know what happened to him?"

"Not specifically."

"He was murdered."

"And Sergeant Church blames Reacher?"

I nodded. "Sergeant Church believes Reacher is the enemy."

CHAPTER THIRTY-FOUR

WE WATCHED AS SHERIFF Taylor interrogated Sergeant Church. He'd come in voluntarily when he heard about the BOLO on base. As I'd expected, the interrogation was short.

He admitted he'd killed Summer. He accused her of corruption and hypocrisy and sending a fine officer like Matthew Clifton to his death, exactly as I'd surmised.

He also admitted to helping General Clifton commit suicide, which seemed to shock Tony. He hadn't noticed how unnaturally long Church had waited to order a ceasefire at the shooting range that day. Few had, and if they did, they doubted their recollections, figured the horror of those moments had warped their perceptions of the passage of time.

Church said General Clifton refused to die like a criminal.

Tony wanted to believe his brother might have lived if Church had ordered the ceasefire sooner. But I'd been watching closely. General Clifton was already dead the moment he stepped into the live fire on the shooting range. Might as well have slammed into a tanker driving ninety-seven miles an hour.

As it turned out, Church didn't admit he'd been planning to

kill Reacher. Maybe he thought he'd get another chance one of these days. Or maybe he had killed Reacher and disposed of the body already. It was certainly plausible. Time would tell.

But after he admitted killing Summer, his future plans were irrelevant. He'd get the maximum sentence, the death penalty. But he'd die of old age in Leavenworth like other soldiers sentenced to death—the precise fate General Clifton had refused to accept.

There would be no trial for Sergeant Church. The Army didn't want to tarnish the top brass like Summer and Clifton. Church offered no defense, which meant the sentencing could be handled quietly and out of the media spotlight.

Sheriff Taylor, Tony, Gaspar and I gathered at *The Lucky Bar* after we heard Church's confession. Jones joined us back at that table in the corner where the music wasn't quite as overwhelming. She brought over five long-necks and joined us.

"I'm sorry about your brother, Tony." She raised her bottle in a bittersweet salute. "General Clifton was a good man. I was proud to serve under him."

He clinked his long-neck with hers and we all drank, even Gaspar.

Then Jones raised her bottle my way. "You're a damn good cop, Otto. You ain't no bigger than a minute. I confess, I didn't think you had it in you."

I tilted the corner of my mouth up as if her words actually amused me and didn't argue as we raised our bottles and clanked and sipped again.

"Alvin will be back to work tomorrow," she said. "Doc says he's got to take care of that bad wing. But he can do this job okay. We'll all pitch in for the next couple of years until Junior gets out of jail."

"It may not be that long, Maddie," Sheriff Taylor said. "Mayne started the shooting. Junior wasn't totally to blame."

"I'm not blamin' Junior." Jones narrowed her eyes and drove a steely gaze into her beer bottle. "It was Reacher. He's the one shoved that bullet up Mayne's nose. He hadn't done that, Mayne woulda been somewhere else instead of whining after that skinny dancer. Junior wouldn't a needed to defend his daddy. None a this woulda happened."

Everybody shrugged. Tony was right. She was as hard as woodpecker lips. If Reacher knew what was good for him, he'd never come within shooting distance of Sergeant Major Madeline Jones or *The Lucky Bar* again.

Gaspar and I said our farewells and left after one beer. We rode in silence on the drive back to the Raleigh airport. Gaspar must have had other things on his mind. His wife and coming son, maybe, and making sure none of his kids grew up without a father like Sergeant Church had done.

I fired up my laptop and wrote my reports. I added the new things I'd learned about Jack Reacher over the past five days. And what I'd learned about Joe Reacher, too.

Reacher had made enemies in the world. Those enemies were looking for him. Some of them like Sergeant Church had skewed perspectives, to be sure. But like Church, even the crazy ones could have the means to make him pay for the things he'd actually done, as well as the things they rightly or wrongly blamed him for.

But Joe Reacher had been universally loved, it seemed. His ex-wife, West Point and Army colleagues, even young boys he'd befriended had nothing but good words to say about him.

Working as an FBI agent, I didn't run into that kind of positive feedback very often. I'd never heard it about Jack Reacher, except from Joe's ex-wife.

As Tony Clifton had said that first day about himself, the Reacher brothers must also have seen a lot of death and lost friends and family many times over. But the bond between brothers couldn't be severed by death.

Brothers could be as different as night and day. Or they could be as similar as clones, looking the same and behaving in similar if not identical ways. The Reacher brothers seemed to me to be a little of both.

For the first time, Gaspar and I had completed one of these Reacher File assignments without the unsettling feeling that Reacher was constantly watching us from the shadows. Which didn't mean he was or wasn't. Only that I hadn't felt it as I usually did.

The rental car return was up ahead. I almost wished that Sergeant Church had actually found and killed Reacher because, if he had, our assignment would be over and we could get back to our normal lives. I wasn't quite sure how I felt about such an almost-wish, but there was no time to figure out my feelings now.

I typed "the end" and uploaded the two reports, one to the Boss's secure satellite and the longer, more detailed one to my personal server. Paying my insurance premium. Who knew what the Boss or Finlay might have planned for me down the road? Plausible deniability was always at the front of my mind. Like all insurance, I was still hoping I'd never need it.

In my personal report, I concluded that Finlay and Cooper were engaged in a war. That much was clear. Reacher seemed to be the prize, dead or alive, and neither Finlay nor Cooper much cared which. Why they wanted him and what they planned to do when they found him remained unknown.

But Gaspar and I were expendable. Which wasn't news. We'd known that for a while.

Gaspar's wife was not in labor. It wasn't Thanksgiving and I still wasn't entitled to vacation time. So when we got the call from the Boss for our next assignment as we entered the airport, we did what we always do.

The only difference was, now we knew we were heading into enemy territory at the outset. Forewarned is forearmed—or foretold, as my mother would say.

We boarded our flight, Gaspar in 1A and me in 3C. I stowed my bags and yanked my seatbelt tight and pulled out a couple of antacids for takeoff.

Moments before we were asked to turn off our electronic devices, the Boss's phone buzzed in my pocket. I pulled it out and read the text.

"Sergeant J. Church dead. Suicide. Shot in the forehead. Beretta. Nine-millimeter full metal jacket through and through."

Reacher had been watching the whole time and I hadn't seen him.

THE END

FROM LEE CHILD
THE REACHER REPORT:
March 2nd, 2012

THE OTHER BIG NEWS is Diane Capri—a friend of mine—wrote a book revisiting the events of KILLING FLOOR in Margrave, Georgia. She imagines an FBI team tasked to trace Reacher's current-day whereabouts. They begin by interviewing people who knew him—starting out with Roscoe and Finlay. Check out this review: "Oh heck yes! I am in love with this book. I'm a huge Jack Reacher fan. If you don't know Jack (pun intended!) then get thee to the bookstore/wherever you buy your fix and pick up one of the many Jack Reacher books by Lee Child. Heck, pick up all of them. In particular, read Killing Floor. Then come back and read Don't Know Jack. This story picks up the other from the point of view of Kim and Gaspar, FBI agents assigned to build a file on Jack Reacher. The problem is, as anyone who knows Reacher can attest, he lives completely off the grid. No cell phone, no house, no car…he's not tied down. A pretty daunting task, then, wouldn't you say?

First lines: "Just the facts. And not many of them, either. Jack Reacher's file was too stale and too thin to be credible. No human could be as invisible as Reacher appeared to be, whether he was currently above the ground or under it. Either the file had been sanitized, or Reacher was the most off-the-grid paranoid Kim Otto had ever heard of." Right away, I'm sensing who Kim Otto is and I'm delighted that I know something she doesn't. You see, I DO know Jack. And I know he's not paranoid. Not really. I know why he lives as he does, and I know what kind of man he is. I loved having that over Kim and Gaspar. If you haven't read any Reacher novels, then this will feel like a good, solid story in its own right. If you have...oh if you have, then you, too, will feel like you have a one-up on the FBI. It's a fun feeling!

"Kim and Gaspar are sent to Margrave by a mysterious boss who reminds me of Charlie, in Charlie's Angels. You never see him...you hear him. He never gives them all the facts. So they are left with a big pile of nothing. They end up embroiled in a murder case that seems connected to Reacher somehow, but they can't see how. Suffice to say the efforts to find the murderer and Reacher, and not lose their own heads in the process, makes for an entertaining read.

"I love the way the author handled the entire story. The pacing is dead on (ok another pun intended), the story is full of twists and turns like a Reacher novel would be, but it's another viewpoint of a Reacher story. It's an outside-in approach to Reacher.

"You might be asking, do they find him? Do they finally meet the infamous Jack Reacher?

"Go...read...now...find out!"

Sounds great, right? Check out *Don't Know Jack*, and let me know what you think.

So that's it for now...again, thanks for reading THE AFFAIR, and I hope you'll like A WANTED MAN just as much in September.

Lee Child

ABOUT THE AUTHOR

Diane Capri is a *New York Times*, *USA Today*, and worldwide bestselling author.

She's a recovering lawyer and snowbird who divides her time between Florida and Michigan. An active member of Mystery Writers of America, Author's Guild, International Thriller Writers, Alliance of Independent Authors, and Sisters in Crime, she loves to hear from readers and is hard at work on her next novel.

Please connect with her online:

http://www.DianeCapri.com

Twitter: http://twitter.com/@DianeCapri
Facebook: http://www.facebook.com/Diane.Capri1
http://www.facebook.com/DianeCapriBooks

If you would like to be kept up to date with infrequent email including release dates for Diane Capri books, free offers, gifts, and general information for members only, please sign up for our Diane Capri Crowd mailing list. We don't want to leave you out! Sign up here:

http://dianecapri.com/contact/

Made in the USA
Coppell, TX
11 April 2021

53520997R00146